MOUNTAIN MAN
ODIN BRANNOCK

JESS T. BRYAN

For information contact: info@outlawspublishing.com

Cover Art by Michael Thomas

Cover design by Outlaws Publishing LLC

Published by Outlaws Publishing LLC

October 2024

10 9 8 7 6 5 4 3 2 1

Chapter 1
Dakota Territory, 1865

As early winter snows whipped across the windswept plain of the Dakotas, a bundled rider mounted on a quarter horse cut across the landscape towards the ridge. Curving plumes of snow rose from beneath the speeding hooves as the rider worked his way up for a better view of the landscape. Galloping to a stop, Odin Brannock, took out a pair of binoculars to scan the sky. Something had him feeling uneasy and he wasn't about to give up until he settled his mind about what trouble may lie ahead.

Scanning the horizon, Odin finally saw smoke rising to the East. The wind buffeted him and his coyote companion, Dusty. Odin prodded Thor and the trio began working their way further up the ridge to better see the smokey-filled area of sky. Thor shifted and moaned nervously beneath him as he nosed the animal close to the ridge. The coyote, too, perked up his ears and paused.

"Dusty, Old Buddy?" asked Odin. "I don't see anything out of the ordinary." Odin reined back on the obviously nervous horse and patted him on the head to calm him down.

"Hey, steady Thor. What's the matter? You smell something?" asked Odin. Spinning around in his saddle looking all around to see what was spooking Thor, Odin turned just in time to see a large shadow come bounding over the top of the ridge directly at them. The monstrous growl gave away the grizzly's intention immediately. The bear lunged at the horse ferociously as it reared up to kick at the attacker.

Odin's heart froze as he immediately thought of the grizzly that had killed his brother not that long ago. The one that had gotten away with murder that still plagued his nightmares. Scar.

Odin hollered as he tried to stay in the saddle. Dusty barked and growled trying to frighten off Scar. Thor, terrified, kicked and reared out of control. As Odin reached for his pistol, a huge claw swatted him hard in the face, throwing him to the ground, unconscious. Thor's terrified screams pierced the cold air as the snow began blowing harder on the ridge. Without Odin holding the reins, Thor ran off as a shot rang in the air. Dusty relentlessly bit and jumped at the mighty beast regardless.

With a closer shot flying past the bear, a lone figure riding a Blue Roan raced through the hostile vastness of snow and cold. Running at full gallop, the rider's voice pierced the freezing air with a shout.

"I'll see you in hell, you blasted fleabag!" Came the strong voice. The mighty grizzly ran past the prone Odin and escaped another rifle shot. Realizing that someone was lying in the snow, the stalwart figure stopped to help. Dusty chased after the bear.

Jolly Hammer swung off his horse and pulled back his coonskin cap to gather himself, exposing his blue eyes and curly gray hair. The wind dropped just enough to let things clear and he tried to determine, through all the blood, if the prone figure was still alive. Dusty returned to protect Odin, furiously barking at the older man.

"All right, don't lose your temper," Jolly told the coyote. Glancing around to make sure the bear hadn't circled back, he realized with the fading light that night was beginning to fall on the snowy plain. Bending down, he determined there was still breath in the giant of a man and began to try to uncover more of his head to see how bad the injuries were.

Cradling him in his arms, Jolly's concern grew when he pushed enough winter coverings away to realize the man was his friend, Odin Brannock. He began to shake him urgently.

"Odin? Odin! Don't do this, Brannock. Come on," said Jolly. With no response, Jolly began frantically rubbing and slapping Odin's unconscious face. The coyote barked and jumped around him as the wind picked back up. Jolly knew they were too exposed to stay there as the bear wouldn't wait forever before doubling back on them.

"Damn, Odin, I didn't realize how big of a man you really are," Jolly muttered under his breath, struggling to lift the larger man. Dragging Odin to his waiting horse, he labored to push the mighty form up onto Shawnee's back. His horse, sensing the danger of the bear had passed, waited patiently for his master to load the precious cargo.

"Gotta get your sorry arse indoors," said Jolly. Odin began a series of moans as the two rode away slowly. Jolly couldn't help but feel shame in causing the whole episode. Had he not pushed the bear towards the ridge, he wouldn't have blindsided an innocent man with the dangerous beast.

"Hang on, Brannock," said Jolly, his voice steady despite the shadows that loomed around them. He kicked his horse's ribs gently, urging it forward. Dusty trotted alongside him, his eyes sharp and scanning the dark terrain before them. The night was bitter, a chill settling in the air as they rode deeper into the unknown.

****

Reaching Jolly's mountain cabin, the older man withdrew on the reins causing Shawnee to come to a halt. The cabin, carved into the rugged landscape of the Dakota hills, was built from rough, unrefined logs weathered over many seasons. Its slanted roof, made of uneven wooden shingles and lined with moss and lichen gave it a timeworn appearance. The structure leaned slightly, a testament to its age and the relentless winds that whipped through the hills.

Inside, the air was thick with the scent of wood-smoke and the earthy aroma of damp soil. A crude stone fireplace dominated one wall, with a blackened chimney that channeled smoke into the sky. The dirt floor was uneven. A worn, handmade table occupied the center, surrounded by mismatched stools and a few burlap sacks used for storage.

"Let's get you inside before you freeze to death," said Jolly as he stepped down from the stirrups. He had a difficult time getting Odin down without causing him more pain. Eventually, he got him off of Shawnee and drug him indoors, followed by Dusty wagging his tail. He helped flop Odin down onto his bed and began doctoring with what little he had.

"There's really nothing more we can do," he told Dusty after washing and examining Odin's face. The claw hadn't done damage to his eye and Jolly figured the big man had hurt himself worse falling to the ground more than anything.

Jolly turned to go back outside to fetch some firewood as Dusty mournfully kept his vigil. The wind was blowing quite strong and the fire needed to be kept going. Dusty stood upon his hind legs pressing down on Odin's chest inside the dark entrance to Jolly's home waiting for a sign of Odin's recovery. Within minutes, Jolly returned with a armful of wood as he shivered in the cold. Banking the fire, he worked on some food to prepare for both of them.

The night wore on, with Jolly falling asleep by the fire. When Odin came to in the cabin bed, Dusty was first to notice the movement. He eagerly pushed his muzzle into Odin's limp hand. Odin couldn't make out the man by the fire through his swollen eye and foggy mind, but felt that he and his friend were safe. Sleep overtook him once again as the Dakota winds moaned outside.

****

The next morning, Odin came to when he realized sunlight was beaming into the room. Sitting up weakly in Jolly's bed, his face clearly showed the terrible wounds from the grizzly's attack. Seeing that his coat and boots had been removed, he surveyed the cabin, which was unkempt but warm and secure. Wracking his brain, he tried to remember what happened after Thor threw him from the saddle. Feeling his head, he could tell his was bruised but nothing was broken.

Jolly and Dusty entered the cabin with fresh firewood. Seeing Odin was up, Dusty growled a friendly greeting. The two men's eyes met and the older was glad to see that the younger had his wits about him and recognized him.

"How are you feeling?" asked Jolly.

"Feeling real lucky, thanks to you," said Odin smiling.

He looked at his friend with a big, devilish grin. Though it had been a few years since they had seen each other, they had not grown apart. Jolly returned the smile.

"So tell me what were you doing out there, anyway?" asked Jolly.

"I thought I saw smoke. I was trying to tell if it was coming from Snakefist's village. That was till that Griz found me," said Odin feeling his face. "I owe you."

"No, don't say that. I was tracking him and didn't realize you were on the other side of that ridge. Just glad I got there in time or he would've finished the job." The older man explained. "Looks like I've managed to keep you around for a little while longer." They both paused as Jolly served up some mash and biscuits he had been warming by the fire. He was glad to see Odin eat, realizing the attack hadn't been as bad as he had thought the night before.

"Said you saw smoke coming from Snakefist? Well, I wouldn't be caught dead there, with all the scalp hunters running loose these days," said Jolly as he finished his biscuit.

"Scalp hunters, you say?" asked Odin standing up for the first time.

"Yeah, scalp hunters been pushing through this area the past few months. Word at the trading post was they're warring with any tribe they come across. I 'spec if you think the smoke was coming from the village, there might have been trouble there," said Jolly.

"I 'spec we better go up there and warn them. Don't you think?" said Odin.

"Hold on! You're not exactly healed overnight you know. Even if they were up there looking for Snakefist, his braves would surely…" started Jolly.

"That's what bothers me, Jolly, I can't sit by and let Snakefist get slaughtered. He's been right good to me," said Odin.

"Oh yes, I bet you can't. After all it's been what? Five or six years since you saw her?" asked Jolly.

"Her who?" asked Odin.

"You know very well, who. Hyacinth, that's who. Snakefist's daughter. You know for a hermit, you don't know a lot," said Jolly with a sly grin.

"I'm sure she's forgotten me by now, that was six years ago," said Odin. Jolly shook his head no.

"Not what I heard. She thinks of you quite a lot, you should've married her or at least cut her out. That way she would have time to mourn you and then marry some buck," said Jolly.

"Got an extra fringe leather shirt I could use? Mine's a bit tore," said Odin, quickly changing the subject. Jolly dug through an old trunk and found him something to wear.

"You're not even listening, are ya?" asked Jolly.

"Nope, I already told ya, it's Snakefist that I'm worried about not Hyacinth. You think she's still with him?" asked Odin.

"Hah! I knew it. As far as I know she is," said Jolly. Odin pulled on the leather fringe shirt, adjusting it to his size. He had one thing on his mind and that was to get going and verify if the village was under attack or not. The smoke had been too much to deny.

"Dusty, we're going out again," said Odin to his furry little friend.

"You're a fool, Odin Brannock!" Jolly got right in Odin's face and the two stared at each other for a moment. Then the older man's face softened. "And, I reckon I'm a bigger fool for going with ya," he finally said.

"First you need a horse, but all I've got out back's two mules. Don't like dogs though," said Jolly.

"No, taint ya got anything else?" asked Odin.

"I'm running a home here, Odin, not a orphanage for horses," sarcastically Jolly.

"No mules of any kind, Jolly! Now what else have you got?" asked Odin, walking to the door of the cabin. Stepping outside, he stretched to feel how sore he was. A beautiful roan was tied up out front.

"What's this one?" asked Odin.

9

"That's my horse, your looking at," said Jolly.

"Fine. I'll take the mule and it better not buck me off, Jolly, or I'll shoot ya," said Odin, rubbing his sore neck.

"You got yourself a deal," said Jolly shaking his old friend's hand.

"I miss my old horse," said Odin as he walked back inside to get his hat.

"Would you just forget about him? We got some dust to make," said Jolly.

****

In the heart of the unforgiving winter landscape, Odin Brannock, Jolly Hammer and his trusty coyote, Dusty, ventured deeper into the rugged valley, on their way to the Sioux village to warn them of scalp hunters on the prowl. Their breath formed misty clouds in the icy air as they rode. The snowflakes danced around them, settling on Dusty's fur and Odin's and Jolly's weathered bear hide coats. As they trudged through the rocky terrain back to the plain, the silence of the valley was broken by the haunting sound of a distant bugle.

"You old skint-flint, you hear that? It sounds like it's coming from Snakefist's village," said Odin.

Odin's piercing blue eyes met Dusty's amber gaze, a silent understanding passing between them. Without a word, they set off towards the source of the mysterious melody, their horse and mule hooves leaving a trail in the freshly fallen snow. The valley seemed to stretch endlessly before them, the towering cliffs casting long shadows in the dim light of the winter morning. As they ascended a steep incline, the bugle call grew louder, echoing off the rocky walls. Odin's heart quickened with anticipation; his curiosity piqued by the unknown origin of the sound. Dusty trotted faithfully by his side, the coyote's keen senses alert to any potential danger.

Finally, as they reached the crest of the valley, a breathtaking sight unfolded before them - Snakefist's village; a Sioux village, dusted with snow, fire and smoke. And among the ruins of the village were bodies that sent a shock-wave shivering up the men's spines.

There, lying on the ground were the remaining villagers of the Sioux Nation, slaughtered and scalped. Bodies were mercilessly scattered all over the ground. All the men, women and braves that came to resist the scalp hunters were dead.

Odin stepped down from his mule, and proceeded to look around for some type of evidence as to who had done this. His gut clenched as the sights sickened him. His feet began to move faster in spite of the pain in his head. All he could think of was finding her, alive. Odin couldn't stand the thought of knowing she had suffered such a fate while he had been laid up.

Chapter 2

Finally, behind Snakefist's teepee, was Snakefist's daughter, Hyacinth. Half hidden in the weeds, she had a bullet piercing her back. Odin's heart sank and he felt he couldn't catch his breath.

Though it had been years since seeing her, time stood still and he felt himself get sick inside, knowing he would never get to hear her voice again. Creeping closer, his feet heavy like lead, he could finally see her hair was lifted. She was dead and scalped, face down in the snow. Odin turned to Jolly and back to her body. 'I'm so sorry,' he thought to himself, almost as if he could pray to her spirit somehow. He stared at her moccasins, his body shaking. She had almost gotten away.

He had been unable to save her. Odin's jaw clenched in rage as his breath came quicker. His fists clenched and he stared at her lying there, helpless. All he knew was he needed to see every last scalper face down on the ground to avenge what they had destroyed.

"Why?" Odin whispered, scarcely able to blink or move.

As Jolly was about to answer, he heard some noise coming from within the brush. Jolly whistled for Odin that someone was coming. Figuring it was another scalp hunter come looking over the massacre, they both readied their rifles. Crunching through the brush was none other than Thor. He had blood on his saddle. Odin's rage broke momentarily as relief washed over him upon seeing his own dear horse returning.

"I thought I'd never see you again Thor," said Odin running up to him as he began pulling his rein. The horse nuzzled his arm in clear relief.

"He must've run up here," said Jolly. Just then, they heard another footstep heading toward them.

"If it's a scalp hunter, he's mine!" said Odin through gritted teeth as he stood proudly against the stark backdrop of the wintry landscape. With his rifle pointing in the direction of the footsteps, he cocked back the hammer and took aim and was preparing to open fire when suddenly, a young brave appeared from the underbrush. It was Tatonga, Snakefist's ten-year-old son.

At first, Tatonga believed that Odin and Jolly had committed the carnage that had flooded his village. He ran at them with blood in his eyes wanting Sioux justice. He lifted his arms holding up a tomahawk and screamed a war cry at them.

"Odin, you better do some fancy talking to this boy or someone's bound to get hurt namely -- us," said Jolly nervously.

Odin began speaking in his native dialect to let the boy know that they had nothing to do with the killing and that it was the work of scalp hunters. At first, the boy thought it was all a lie.

"You put that tomahawk down, son, we're not your enemy," said Jolly.

Continuing with Sioux dialect, Odin eventually sway the young brave to lower his weapon.

It sure did took you long enough. Ask him what happened?" asked Jolly.

Odin spoke again, and asked what had happened to his village. He went on stating that most of the young braves were gone hunting, so they didn't know about the attack till it was all over. He went on to say that on a nearby hill, under the vast expanse of a crimson sky, men with guns marched with determination, their boots kicking up clouds of dirt and snow as they led their pack animals forward. The sound of bugles echoed through the valley, a haunting melody that seemed to carry both a sense of urgency and a call to arms.

"Who do you think would've done something like this?" asked Odin.

"Couldn't say, but... what are you asking me, ask the boy?" said Jolly.

"For an army scout, you sure aren't worth a damn," said Odin.

Odin began talking to the boy, who was sad losing his father. The boy sniffed, his eyes were glassy from all the tears that ran down his face. He then turned and spoke to Odin, in the Sioux dialect.

"What he say?" asked Jolly.

"He said among the men, who did this, was a man called Merlin.

He stood out among them because the man's eyes was filled with a mixture of fear and determination. He clutched his rifle tightly, the weight of it a constant reminder of the gravity of the situation they found themselves in," said Odin.

"I don't believe I know a Merlin, but then there's been so many traders moving into the territory its hard to keep track," said Jolly.

"Well the boy can't stay here, he'll have to go with us," said Odin.

"I reckon, but where to, I mean we can't just show up at Fort Lever with a Sioux boy…" started Jolly.

"Don't you think I know that, I have ran out of options," said Odin.

"How about trying to find his next of kin? 'Less you got any other ideas," said Jolly.

"Not by the hair of my whiskers I don't. Just gonna be hard to keep the boy under wraps 'cause not likely he'll be welcome," said Odin.

"Then we just have to make him feel welcome, then, won't we," said Jolly.

****

The sun dipped below the horizon, casting long shadows across the landscape as Odin, Jolly and Tatonga pressed on, their faces set in grim determination. Odin and Jolly picked up a string of pack animals, burdened with supplies and ammunition, plodded along wearily, their breath forming misty clouds in the cool evening air.

Tatonga stole a glance at his comrades, their faces etched with a mixture of exhaustion and resolve. Each step brought them closer to the unknown, to a future shrouded in uncertainty. As night fell and the stars emerged like pinpricks of light in the darkening sky, Tatonga felt a sense of camaraderie among his fellow saviors, a bond forged in the crucible of war. Together, they were a force to be reckoned with, a beacon of hope in a world consumed by chaos.

"Hey, Odin, just thought of something. What are folks gonna say, when we come riding in with a Sioux boy? Mostly likely they're gonna be stung," said Jolly.

"I got that covered. Gonna take him down to the next watering hole and clean him up a bit, and for now on, his name is Challi," sad Odin.

"Challi? Why the name changed?" asked Jolly.

"You wanna start a panic? Folks find out he's Snakefist's son, their bound to be a ruckus," said Odin.

"You got a point there. Just had another thought, suppose we run into those scalp hunters before we reach Fort Lever, what then?" asked Jolly.

"For an old guy you sure do do a lot of supposing. We'll deal with them like we would any other animal. Kill 'em," said Odin.

"Just that I'm worried about the boy that's all. Don't want nothing to happen to the little squirt," said Jolly.

"Let's keep riding, we're nearly to the next watering hole," said Odin.

After reaching the next water hole, Odin, Jolly, and Challi stepped down from their horses and mule and preceded to take Challi and bathe him. For he had an odor in a half. Mustn't had a bath in a month or two. Challi began a series of Sioux dialect, as he began to slowly back away from the water hole.

"No use fightin' Son, you need a bath," said Jolly.

Finally, after scrapping with the boy to take a bath, Odin walked up to him and picked him up and bopped him in. Odin wasn't gonna take no for an answer. Odin reached into Thor's saddlebags and pulled out a bar of soap and began scrubbing the boy. Clothes and all. But not before Challi dragged Odin in with him. Jolly turned just in the nick of time to see Odin go in.

"Gee Odin, didn't know it was Saturday already," laughed Jolly.

"Oh, no," said Odin.

As Jolly reached for Odin's hand to pull him out, both Odin and Challi pulled him in with them.

"Now nobody said I needed a bath," said Jolly.

After splashing in the water hole, they all heard a horse coming toward them. The men and Challi stepped out of the water and preceded to stand next to the horses and mule. Approaching them, a rider came close and pulled back on his reins.

"Thought I'd take a drink of this here water, hope it's not polluted," said the rider.

Challi began a series of Sioux dialect that only Odin understood.

"Naw you go right ahead, what's your name son?" asked Jolly.

"Name's Perkins," said the rider.

"Perkins? Uh, I don't believe I know a Perkins. Must be new to the territory," said Jolly.

Perkins as he was calling himself, stepped down and began filing his canteen with water.

"What brings you all the way out here, don't mind me asking?" asked Jolly.

"Me and some of my friends, were out scouting and... I ran on ahead scouting for some water. Where might you folks be heading?" asked Perkins.

"We're heading for Fort Lever," said Odin.

Challi didn't like Perkins. He began a series of Sioux dialect and began pointing in an angry tone to Odin and Jolly. Odin took notice.

Jolly noticed his saddlebags were full of something and flies bad begun buzzing. They continued to watch Perkins.

"Much oblige for the water," said Perkins.

"Whatcha you got in your saddlebags, Son. Flies are swarming all over the place," said Jolly resting his hand on his Colt Navy pistol handle.

"Oh, that, that's nothing than spoiled meat, I picked up on the trail," said Perkins.

"Boy, whatcha go in that saddlebag? I think your lying," said Odin.

Chapter 3

"I done told you mister, it's spoiled deer meat I found on the trail," said nervously Perkins.

"Your lying, their scalps. Sioux scalps ain't they?" asked Odin.

Challi began ranting in Sioux and jerked out a knife.

"Mister I don't know what you're talking about," said Perkins.

"You see this here boy belongs to Chief Snakefist. Saw the whole thing. And he tells me that your name isn't Perkins. And that your friends and you were at a Sioux village not more than five hours ago," said Odin.

"You gonna take my word for it or that Indian brat's?" asked Perkins.

"I most certainly am. You murdering trash! You butchered his entire family," said Odin.

"Okay, name's not Perkins. Name's Merlin and I didn't do nothing," said Merlin.

"And you didn't help 'em either," said Odin.

Jolly stood and held Challi back. The boy wanted revenge. Odin reached for his Colt 1851 Navy .36 caliber and cocked the hammer back.

"You can't do this! For a bunch of Injuns? They're not even human," said Merlin.

"'Fore I kill you, I want the names of the others," said Odin.

"Good luck old man, my friend's hear the shot, they'll come running and kill you both and that Indian brat," said Merlin.

"We'll see about that. Names!" demanded Odin.

"Better do what he says Son, Ol' Odin doesn't play when it comes to killing folks," said Jolly.

"You have until a count of three," said Odin.

"I t'aint no snitch," said Merlin.

"One…" started Odin.

"You won't kill me," said Merlin.

"Two…" continued Odin.

Odin shifted his Colt Navy and fired striking the young man in the knee.

"Next's in your head. Talk!" said Odin.

"Alright! I'll talk first you gotta get me to a doctor, I'm bleeding badly," said Merlin.

"Naw you'll live. Better answer the man son, while he still in a good enough humor," said Jolly.

"There's ten of us," said Merlin.

"Wrong answer," said Odin. As he fired another round into the man's other knee.

"I don't care how many, I just want names, come on Merlin!" said Odin.

"The… the Grim brothers," said Merlin.

"Digger and Hawk Grim; should've known," said Jolly.

"Who else!" asked Odin.

"Screw you!" said Merlin.

Odin cocked the hammer back on his Colt Navy and fired another shot this time he fired a shot and it wound up in the man's head.

"Now what?" asked Jolly.

"Quit your yammering! We gotta haul outta here, before those ten come looking for their missing buddy," said Odin.

"Not much to go on, we know that there's ten men out there somewheres that has Sioux scalps and two of them are the Grim brothers.

I don't like it. No sir, I don't like it one bit," said Jolly.

"What choice have we got? We gotta head for Fort Lever. That's our only sanctuary," said Odin.

As Odin, Jolly and Challi followed Dusty into the thicket of trees, the air grew thick with tension. The dense foliage cast eerie shadows, the only sound the rustling of leaves in the cold wind. Odin's heart pounded in his chest as he navigated through the maze of branches, his senses heightened by the adrenaline coursing through his veins. The pistol shots continued to echo in the distance, a grim reminder of the danger lurking nearby. After hearing the shots, Merlin's friends perked their ears up and immediately knew something was wrong.

"What was that? Sound like pistol firing, Merlin must be in trouble," said Hawk.

"Merlin is always in trouble I told you not to bring him, now we gotta see what's happened to him," said Digger.

They immediately dropped everything and ran back toward their horses, as fast as their legs could carry them. Digger and Hawk Grim along with nine men got mounted and rode off toward the pistol shots.

****

Dusty's barks pierced through the silence, leading the three deeper into the forest's heart. The trees seemed to close in around them, their twisted branches reaching out like gnarled fingers. The air was thick with the scent of damp earth and moss, a reminder of the rain that had drenched the forest just days before. Jolly trudged behind Odin, his brow furrowed in confusion. "I sure hope you know where you're going. I thought Fort Lever was in the other direction," he said, glancing back at the path they had left behind.

"Taking a shortcut," replied Odin with a shrug, his confidence unwavering despite the encroaching shadows that danced among the underbrush. Dusty darted ahead, his tail wagging with excitement as if he were aware of a secret that the others were not. Jolly couldn't shake the feeling of unease that gripped him. The forest was alive with sounds—the rustling leaves, the distant call of a bird—but it felt like they were intruding, trespassing in a realm that thrived without them.

As they ventured deeper, the light began to fade, and the trees grew taller and thicker, their trunks towering like ancient sentinels. Jolly could feel the coolness of the evening settling in, and he quickened his pace, wanting to keep close to Odin. "Are you sure this is the right way?" he pressed again, his voice tinged with worry. Dusty paused and looked back at them, as if gauging their resolve, then resumed his exploration of the forest floor, sniffing at every intriguing scent.

Odin, sensing Jolly's anxiety, stopped to reassure him. "Relax, we'll find it. Dusty is leading us. He knows things we don't," he said, watching as the coyote bounded away, chasing after a flickering firefly. The forest's ambiance shifted, becoming eerily quiet as if waiting for something to happen. Just then, Dusty came to a sudden halt, staring intently at a cluster of bushes. Jolly and Odin exchanged a glance, curiosity piquing their interest.

With a cautious approach, they moved to Dusty's side. As they parted the foliage, a hidden trail emerged, barely visible beneath the undergrowth. A flicker of hope igniting within him. They stepped onto the path, feeling a renewed sense of purpose. Perhaps this shortcut would lead them to Fort Lever after all, and as they followed Dusty down the narrow trail, the darkness of the forest seemed less daunting.

"What did you find, boy?" he whispered, stepping cautiously towards his companion. As they moved to Dusty's side, they parted the thick foliage, revealing a narrow trail hidden beneath a carpet of leaves. The path was faint, barely noticeable, but it seemed to beckon them forward. "Looks like he found something," Jolly said, his voice steady despite the uncertainty that lingered in the air. The idea of a shortcut filled him with renewed purpose; perhaps this would lead them to Fort Lever after all.

With a deep breath, Jolly stepped onto the path, the crunch of twigs underfoot providing a reassuring sound against the silence of the forest. Dusty trotted ahead, his nose to the ground, guiding Jolly deeper into the woods. The towering trees loomed overhead, their leaves whispering secrets to one another, but with Dusty by his side, the darkness felt less intimidating.

As they ventured further, the trail twisted and turned, leading them through thickets of brambles and patches of sunlight that danced upon the ground. Jolly kept his eyes peeled, looking for signs that they were on the right track. Dusty paused occasionally, ears perkcd, as if sensing something just beyond the reach of their vision. Jolly felt a thrill of excitement mixed with a touch of trepidation; the forest was alive, and every sound seemed to echo with the promise of what lay ahead.

Odin had always sought solace in the dense woods that blanketed his home, the towering trees standing like ancient sentinels against the passage of time. Yet, this day, as he meandered along a familiar trail, he stumbled upon something unexpected—a clearing that held the very men he was looking for. The scalp hunters led by Digger came face to face with Odin and Jolly. Challi raised his little finger and began shouting in Sioux that they were the ones that attacked his village.

"Challi, you go find yourself a perch and stay there, we'll handle this," said Odin.

Challi did as he was told. And trotted away.

"Well, well, well, if ain't Brannock. Nice to see you again," said Hawk.

"Funny we can't say the same," said Jolly.

"What's you got with ya, an Indian boy?" asked Digger.

"Yeah and we aim to take him to his people, and nobody's gonna stop us either," said Odin.

"Just how you gonna do that? Theirs ten of us, and only two of you," said Hawk.

"We'll manage," said Jolly.

"I don't suppose any of y'all wanna surrender?" asked Odin.

"Now that's funny, coming from a hillbilly mountain goat such as yourself. You might wanna repeat that, Brannock, don't think my men heard you," said Digger.

"They heard. But in case they didn't…" said Odin he raised his Henry rifle and fired.

"That plain enough for ya!" shouted Jolly.

Challi wasn't about to let the men go unpunished, for the death of his father. He was seeking Sioux justice. Still carrying a bow, he pull an arrow from behind his back and pulled it tight aiming it directly at one of the men on horseback. He released it into the air, where it found itself in the chest of the one of the scalp hunters. He pitched forward causing the man to fall from his horse. Dead.

The scalp hunters reached for their rifles and began firing at Challi, but the boy was too far out of range. The serene beauty of nature was shattered by the cacophony of gunfire and the anguished cries of men locked in a brutal struggle. His heart raced as he realized the scene before him: Digger, the notorious scalp hunter leader, was locked in combat with Odin and Jolly.

As the smoke hung thick in the air, Odin felt a primal instinct surge within him. He wasn't merely a bystander in this tempest of violence; he was a son of the earth, a protector of his friends. Challi fierce and resolute, fought valiantly beneath the watchful gaze of his elders, an embodiment of wisdom and strength. With every crack of gunfire, Odin's heart ached not just for the bloodshed but for the deep rift that had formed between the tribe. The echoes of his shared past reverberated in his mind— stories of laughter by the fire, shared hunting trips, and the mingling of cultures that felt so distant now.

As the sun dipped below the horizon, casting long shadows, the air crackled with tension. Hawk ducked behind his horse, his heart racing as gunfire echoed around him. "Digger, let's get outta here, uh," he shouted, his voice barely audible above the chaos. The bullets whizzed by, creating a dangerous symphony of destruction. The danger was all too real, and Hawk's instincts screamed for retreat.

Digger, however, was unfazed. He crouched low, peering over his grime-coated horse. "Are you kidding? We got them right where we want them," he replied, his eyes glinting with a fierce determination. He gestured to Cook, who was reloading his weapon nearby. "Cook, take a couple of men, and move in," Digger ordered, his voice steady as he plotted their next move. Hawk stared at Digger in disbelief; it was reckless. But it was too late for second thoughts—the decision had been made.

Cook nodded, a grim smile tugging at his lips as he gathered a few men, each one sharing a look of hard resolve. They crept through the trees, using the broken limbs and boulders as cover. The plan was simple: strike fast and hard, take out the enemy before they even realized what hit them. Hawk felt the weight of uncertainty crushing him as he watched his comrades disappear into the darkness. He wanted to shout a warning, to call them back, but the moment passed. The sound of footsteps and muffled voices filled the air, and soon, the clash of bodies erupted in the night.

Gunshots rang out, and chaos ensued. Digger led the charge, his instincts sharp as he maneuvered through the fray. Hawk was torn between wanting to help and the urge to flee. He could see Cook and the others engaging the enemy, their movements fluid and practiced. But every shot fired felt like a countdown, a reminder that each second spent in this hell, could be his last. Just as he was about to make his move, a loud explosion rocked the warehouse, sending debris flying. The ground shook beneath him, and in that split second, everything changed.

Odin spotted Dusty getting into the act too, as he began a series of barks as if his barks were a rifle. Challi the brave's eyes burned with the fire of a thousand ancestors, a testament to the honor and struggle of his people. Digger, with his ruthless ambition, seemed oblivious to the weight of history that pressed down upon them.

As the dust settled, Hawk blinked in disbelief. Digger was on the ground, wounded but alive, and Cook was nowhere to be seen midst the chaos. The fight had taken a turn, and Hawk knew in that moment that survival now hinged on a single decision. He rushed towards Digger, determination burning in his chest. "We're getting out of here, now!" he yelled, grabbing Digger's arm. With the sounds of battle still echoing in the air, Hawk knew they had to escape, but the question lingered: would they make it out alive, or had the night already claimed them?

Jolly managed to fire at the oncoming advances from the scalp hunters. Killing two or three at a time. The next thing, Jolly knew he was on the ground, blood spurting from his shoulder. Challi raced toward Jolly and began closing up the wound as fast as he could. Dusty charged down the hill toward Jolly as if he could help him in some way. The seven men tore back down the hill escaping the rifle shots as best as they could. Meeting back up with Digger and Hawk.

"You ain't seen the last of us, Brannock!" shouted Digger.

Odin's feet moved before his mind could catch up; he plunged into the fray, a primal cry erupting from his throat. His presence was a sudden gust of wind in the storm, a figure that momentarily froze the chaos around him. Digger turned, his face contorted in disbelief.

"This over a few mingy scalps," said Digger spatting, venom lacing words.

Odin's heart was unwavering. "I side with blood, Digger," said Odin.

"You won't ever reach Fort Lever, I swear to it!" shouted Digger.

Digger, Hawk and the rest of the men gathered their horses and stepped up in their stirrups and galloped away as fast as they could possibly go. With a fierce resolve, Odin stepped forward, positioning himself between Digger and Challi. "This isn't the Sioux way," he implored, his voice rising over the tumult. Odin, sensing an opportunity, approached Jolly cautiously, the wisdom of ages in his eyes. "Let' em go, they'll be back," said Odin.

Challi began a series of Sioux dialect.

"What he say?" asked Jolly who was able enough to get up and walk toward a nearby stone and sat down.

"He says this land belongs to all who walk upon it, and bloodshed only begets more bloodshed," said Odin.

The words hung in the air, a fragile bridge across the chasm between them, and for a moment, the chaos ebbed as all sides hesitated. The clearing, once a battlefield, transformed into a crucible for change. Challi, caught between fury and familial bonds, faltered. Odin stepped forward, placing a hand on the young brave's shoulder.

"We are stronger together, Challi. Let us honor the spirits of your ancestors by choosing peace over war," said Odin.

****

As the sun began to dip below the horizon, casting a golden hue over the clearing.

"How many men have we lost?" asked Digger.

"Nine. We're down to seven Digger. Hey let's sic the army on them Digger," said Hawk.

"You fool, can't sic the army on them, because of that army scout Jolly. They know his reputation and wouldn't dare not believe him that it was us that did them scalping. Gotta think of something," said Digger.

****

In that twilight moment, the echoes of history whispered promises of unity, and Odin felt the weight of the world lift slightly, a flicker of hope igniting in the hearts of those who had come to fight but found a reason to stand together instead. Odin began scratching his full bushy beard. As Jolly watched, torn between loyalty to his friends and a growing sense of unease, he saw Dusty emerge from the shadows, a determined glint in his eyes.

"Well, what do you suppose we do now?" asked Jolly.

"Gotta get you to a doctor and let him take that slug out of your shoulder," said Odin.

Odin made a choice that would forever alter the course of his destiny.

"Not me, Odin, I was referring about the current situation. Do we ride for Fort Lever or what?" asked Jolly who was rubbing his shot-up shoulder.

With a deep breath, Odin followed Dusty who trotted up to Jolly and began licking his face.

"Would you please tell him to stop that? No tellin' where his tongue's been. Probably licking his balls. Get away," said Jolly.

Chapter 4

Odin ignoring him as Dusty continued to lick Jolly in the face.

"There's a town not far from here, you think you can make it old man?" asked Odin.

"Just who are you calling old man?" asked Jolly.

"You. Now let's get going before those scalp hunters return," said Odin.

"I've whipped more Injuns than you've ever been seen," said Jolly rising up from the stone he was sitting on.

"Can you ride? Or do we have to tote ya," said Odin.

"I can ride, just get me on Shawnee and see who gets left behind," said Jolly dragging his feet as he approached Shawnee.

"Take your time, night's approaching," said Odin.

"Why don't you shut up," replied Jolly.

Jolly stepped up into the stirrups and swung up, grunting in pain as he swung up.

"You ready now?" asked Odin.

"I'll ride when I please," said Jolly.

Their resolve strengthened as they prepared to face whatever lay ahead. The echoes of Digger's last words reverberated in Odin's mind, a haunting reminder of the sacrifices made in the name of honor.

"Let's go," said Odin waving his arm in a move out position.

"So how far, is this town of yours and will there be a saloon?" asked Jolly.

Odin's voice was steady but laced with urgency. "Red Clay is eighteen miles from here. As for the saloon, you're not going there to drink. You're going to see a doctor to get that bullet out of you. Challi and I can do only so much." He glanced at Jolly who was riding slumped over Shawnee's saddle, blood seeping through his shirt. The sun hung low in the sky, casting long shadows that danced across the dusty floor of their hideout, a makeshift shelter hidden away from the prying eyes of the world.

Challi moved closer, his brow furrowed in concern. He had seen too many men succumb to their wounds, and he wasn't about to let another one slip away. Challi spoke in Sioux, he urged, his voice soft but firm. The elder man, eyes glazed with pain, nodded slowly, understanding the gravity of his situation. He knew he had to trust them; they were his only chance at survival.

****

Red Clay, Dakota Territory

As they made their way toward Red Clay, the landscape shifted from barren desert to the rugged hills that surrounded the town. The sun dipped lower, painting the sky in hues of orange and purple. Odin kept a steady pace on Thor while Challi continued to ride the mare mule, Dusty trotted alongside them, Challi scanned for any signs of danger. They reached the saloon, its welcoming sight. But they had no time for the drinks or laughter that echoed from within; there was a doctor waiting to pull the bullet from the old man's shoulder.

Dusty's ears perked up as he caught a whiff of something unusual in the air. The loyal coyote, with his keen senses, began to sniff intently, signaling to Odin, Jolly, and Challi, that trouble was brewing nearby. The bustling town, filled with vendors shouting their wares and children laughing, suddenly fell into a tense hush as the three friends turned in their saddles. Their eyes scanned the crowd, searching for any signs of danger lurking among the stalls of fruits and spices.

Suddenly, from the corner of Odin's eye, a shadowy figure slipped out from behind a stack of crates. Odin's heart raced as he recognized the silhouette; it was a man he had hoped never to see again. The figure's billowed in the wind, and a sinister grin spread across his face as he scanned the market. Jolly tightened his grip on the reins, and Challi's ears perked up, sensing the shift in the atmosphere. Dusty let out a low growl, ready to protect his friends.

As the figure stepped closer, the crowd began to part, revealing him in all his menacing glory. Odin felt a rush

of adrenaline surge through him. He remembered the
tales of this man's treachery, the chaos he had brought to
their village before. Jolly's voice broke through the
silence, urging everyone to stay calm while he and Odin
plotted their next move. Challi, ever the brave one, stood
tall beside them, ready to face whatever danger
approached.

The shadowy figure finally stopped, standing just a
few paces away. With a theatrical flourish, he revealed a
familiar face— Milo Devereux, once a trusted ally, now
turned rogue. The French fur trader on occasion, a well-
known thief who gets people drunk and takes their
money after they pass out.

The tension in the air grew thick as an impending
storm, and the friends exchanged worried glances. Dusty
sniffed the ground, sensing the dread that loomed as they
prepared to confront Odin's old enemy. The town, once
vibrant and lively, now felt like a battleground about to
erupt as choices hung heavy in the air.

"Whoa, Dusty, come back boy! Stop! Stop! Stop!"
Odin yelled, his voice tinged with urgency as Dusty
hesitated, torn between loyalty to his master and the
instinct to flee.

With a yip of alarm, Dusty darted back to Odin's side
a few minutes later, his tail tucked between his legs as
Milo loomed closer, his presence suffocating in the dim
light. As Odin braced himself for the inevitable

confrontation, he knew that their bond would be tested like never before in the face of this unpredictable foe.

"Crazy coyote! You might have gotten yourself killed," Odin whispered, his heart pounding with worry as he embraced his loyal companion.

"What about the doc?" asked Jolly.

"He can wait, you ain't dying. This can't," said Odin.

No sooner than said that, Milo turned toward Odin's direction and without missing a beat, he started to laugh. A big hardy laugh. Milo leaned casually against the bar, his thick French accent cutting through the noise of the bustling saloon. "Well, well. My American friends, Jolly and Odin. How you been?" he asked, a mischievous glint in his eyes. Jolly, with his bright smile, raised his glass in greeting. Odin, more reserved but equally intrigued, nodded in acknowledgment, his gaze shifting from Milo to the busy street outside.

Milo noticed that Jolly was cantering his shoulder.

"Doing alright," said Jolly gripping his shoulder.

"What happened to you?" asked Milo looking at Jolly and his shoulder.

"I got s…" started Jolly.

"Bucked. He got bucked off, but he'll be alright. Gonna see the local doc if this here town has one?" asked Odin.

"Red Clay has a doctor, he's up the street ways, care if I walk along with ya?" asked Milo.

"Yes... I mean no, we can talk over old times," said Odin.

The three friends had met during a whirlwind summer in Quebec, their lives intertwined by chance and shared adventures. They had explored the cobbled streets, indulged in rich pastries, and marveled at the beauty of the city. Now, months later, they found themselves reunited in a cozy corner of an American saloon, where the aroma of freshly brewed coffee mingled with the laughter of patrons. The atmosphere buzzed with warmth, and the bond between them felt just as strong as when they first met.

Milo's stories were always a spectacle, filled with humor and a flair for the dramatic. As he recounted his latest escapades in Canada, Jolly and Odin listened intently, occasionally interjecting with laughter. The conversation flowed effortlessly, as if no time had passed since their last encounter. They reminisced about the fur trapping business, the vibrant markets, and the late-night discussions over glasses of wine, each memory adding another layer to their friendship.

As the sun began to set, casting a golden hue through the saloon windows, Jolly glanced at his pocket watch. "We should do this more often," he said, a hint of longing in his voice. Odin nodded in agreement, his expression thoughtful. The distance between them was more than just miles; it was the life paths they had chosen. Yet, in that moment, they felt a renewed sense of connection, a promise that their friendship would endure despite the challenges of life.

"To memories and new adventures," Milo declared, his accent thick with emotion.

"To new adventures," Odin and Jolly said in unison.

Challi didn't care for Milo, neither did Dusty. Milo turned and walked away. Eventually, they came to the medical office. Under the plaque it read John Barry, M. D.

"I better knock, I suppose," said Odin.

Odin knocked hard on the door. John heard the knock from within and waddled on over to the front door. John Barry, a grizzled man with wise eyes and steady hands, was already preparing his instruments when they burst through the door. "I see you've brought me a patient. Lay him down," he instructed, his voice calm and authoritative. Challi assisted as Odin carefully placed Jolly on the examination table. The doctor wasted no time, his fingers deftly assessing the wound, ready to mend what had been broken. The world outside faded away as the procedure began, hope threading its way into Jolly's heart.

As Doc Barry worked, Odin and Challi stood vigil, the weight of their journey evident in their tired expressions. They had faced danger, fought through chaos, and now, they were on the cusp of victory. The bullet would be removed, and life would continue—at least for Jolly. In that moment, the medical office was not just a place of revelry; it was a sanctuary where lives were saved, and friendships were forged in the face of adversity.

Odin and Challi stood close, their eyes never leaving Jolly. Each had a story etched into their features, a testament to the trials they had faced together. They had journeyed through perilous territories, encountering dangers that would have broken lesser spirits. But here, in this sanctuary, they were united by a common goal: to see Jolly recover. The weight of their experiences hung heavily on their shoulders, yet they remained steadfast, drawing strength from their shared bond. The flicker of hope in Jolly's eyes reassured them that their sacrifices were not in vain.

As Doc Barry began his work, the atmosphere shifted. With every careful movement, he spoke softly, explaining each step to Odin and Challi. His voice was calm and reassuring, a steady anchor in the storm of emotions swirling around them. "Just a little longer," he said, glancing up with a reassuring smile. Odin clenched his fists, trying to mask the worry etched on his face, while Challi brushed a stray hair from Jolly's forehead, whispering words of encouragement. The room felt alive with the energy of camaraderie and love, a testament to the deep connections formed in the face of adversity.

Moments stretched into what felt like hours, but finally, Doc Barry announced, "It's done." Relief washed over Odin and Challi as they exchanged glances filled with unspoken gratitude. Jolly, though weak, managed a faint smile, his spirit unbroken. The bullet was gone, a physical weight lifted, but far more significant was the emotional bond that had solidified during this ordeal.

The sun hung low in the sky, casting long shadows as Doc squinted, trying to catch a glimpse of the distant horizon. "Where about you are heading?" he asked, his voice a mix of curiosity and concern. The dusty road stretched out before them, a reminder of the rugged journey that lay ahead.

Jolly, always the optimist, grinned as he adjusted his cap. "We're on our way to Fort Lever, Doc, till this happens," he replied, pointing to the hole in his shoulder.

The sun casting a warm glow over the quiet town. Doc looked at Jolly, who sat on the steps, his arm cradled gingerly against his chest. The remnants of a recent scuffle were evident; the bruising was just beginning to take shape around the shoulder. "I wouldn't worry so much about that shoulder. It'll heal in time. As for Fort Lever, why go there?" Doc asked, concern lacing his voice.

Jolly chuckled lightly, a hint of defiance creeping into his tone. "For a grizzled old doctor, you sure do like to ask a lot of questions," he replied, shifting his position slightly to ease the discomfort. His eyes sparkled with mischief, betraying a sense of adventure that had been brewing for some time.

"Just being friendly, I meant no harm," Doc responded, a slight smile breaking through his serious demeanor. He was well aware of the allure that the fort held for the townsfolk.

Jolly stood up, a determined gleam in his eyes. "You worry too much, Doc. Life's too short to sit around nursing old scars. Besides, I have a lead on where they might have stashed some of the old supplies." He took a few steps forward, testing the shoulder, and grimaced slightly but didn't let it deter him. Doc sighed, knowing that once Jolly set his mind to something, no amount of caution could sway him.

"Alright, but you'd better promise to take it easy," Doc conceded, shaking his head with a reluctant grin. "Let's make a deal: you scout the area, and if anything goes sideways, you come back and let me patch you up." Jolly laughed, the sound echoing against the wooden beams, and with that, Jolly and his friends set off toward Fort Lever.

"Jolly, stay put. Challi and I will look for some fresh supplies to take with us to Fort Lever then onward to California," said Odin, adjusting the straps of his pack. The sun hung high in the sky. Dusty wagged his tail, understanding that his friends had important work to do.

Jolly leaned against a weathered rail post, watching his friends, Odin, Challi and Dusty, stroll ahead toward town. The sun hung low in the sky, casting long shadows on the dusty road. Jolly felt a sense of calm as he observed the lively banter between his friends, each step taking them closer to the general store where they hoped to gather some much-needed supplies. He had decided to stay behind, enjoying the quiet of the countryside for just a moment longer.

Challi, with his keen eyes, spotted the general store first. He pointed excitedly, his words flowing in Sioux, a language that resonated with the earth and the wind. Odin, whose brow furrowed slightly, turned to Challi and whispered, "That's it. Challi, don't communicate in Sioux—be silent. I'll explain later." There was a hint of urgency in Odin's tone, a reminder that sometimes, understanding came not just from words but from the context in which they were shared.

As Dusty looked back at Jolly, a smile crept across his face, the kind that spoke of friendship and shared adventures. Jolly waved them on, a silent agreement that he would catch up once he finished savoring these moments of solitude. The town was alive with sounds— the distant laughter of children playing, the clatter of hooves on the dirt and rocky streets—but here, where he stood, the world felt more serene.

Jolly took a deep breath, filling his lungs with the warm air, and allowed himself a small smile. He didn't mind being left behind for a few moments; he knew that soon he would join his friends, and the laughter and stories would come rushing back. For now, he relished the peace, watching as Challi waved enthusiastically at him, their figures growing smaller as they headed toward the general store.

Odin, Dusty, and Challi stepped into the general store owned by Jeremiah Lynch, the scent of fresh produce mingling with the dusty aroma of old wooden shelves. The bell above the door chimed, announcing their arrival. Jeremiah, a stout man with a bushy mustache, glanced up from the counter where he was ringing up a customer. His eyes lit up with recognition as he spotted the trio. "Well, if it isn't Odin! Where's that old skint-flint partner of yours, Jolly. What brings you in today?" he called out, his voice warm and welcoming.

Odin stepped forward, a grin stretching across his face. "Jolly's around. I'm here to grab some supplies," he replied. Challi, bounced on his heels, eager to explore the aisles filled with colorful goods. Odin pulled out a list from his pocket, making sure they wouldn't forget anything essential.

Odin leaned against the weathered counter of Jeremiah's general store, the scent of aged wood and tobacco hanging in the air. "Need three boxes of Colt .36 Navy pistol shells. Need some chaw of tobacco for Jolly," he began, his voice steady but low. Jeremiah nodded and moved towards the back of the store, his worn boots creaking with each step. The sun cast long shadows through the dusty windows, illuminating the dust motes dancing in the air.

With a warm smile spreading across his face Odin watched Challi, curiously eyeing a jar of stick candy. The bright colors of the candy seemed to dance in the afternoon sunlight that filtered through the shop's window. As Odin turned to gather supplies, he noticed Jeremiah sorting through a box of inventory. "Okay, what else can I help you with?" Jeremiah asked, his voice steady and inviting.

With a gentle pat on Challi's head, Odin knelt down to his level. "You've got your eyes on that candy, haven't you?" he said, chuckling softly. Challi nodded eagerly, his bright eyes sparkling with delight. The jar was filled with all sorts of sugary treats, each stick promising a burst of sweetness. Odin felt a rush of affection for the boy, remembering his own childhood days when a simple candy could light up an entire afternoon.

"And a couple of stick candy for the boy," Odin said to Jeremiah, who was now leaning against the counter with a knowing smile. Jeremiah quickly reached for the jar, carefully selecting two colorful sticks. He handed them to Odin, who placed them in Challi's eager little hands.

"There you go! Just for you," he said, watching as Challi's face lit up with joy.

As they exited the store, Challi happily unwrapped one of his candies, the sweet scent enveloping them. Odin chuckled, "Just remember to share, okay?" Challi nodded, his mouth full of sugary goodness. With the sun setting behind them, the two friends walked toward the local saloon, laughter echoing in the soft evening air, the simple joys of friendship and candy sweetening their day.

Challi impatiently pacing. He tugged at his collar and grinned at Odin as he stepped out of the store, his arms full of supplies. Challi spoke in Sioux "You think he's got enough to keep us going?" he joked, his laughter booming in the quiet of the late afternoon. Odin rolled his eyes but couldn't suppress a smile; Jolly's humor was infectious, even if it was often at the expense of common sense. Challi spoke up again in Sioux and asked why where they going to the saloon.

Challi seemed restless. With a furrowed brow, he spoke in Sioux, his words laced with concern. He was not accustomed to the ways of the settlers, and this journey felt uncertain to him. "What about Jolly?" he asked, his gaze darting to the door, as if expecting the absent man to walk in at any moment. Odin assured him he would be fine, Challi couldn't shake the unease that settled in his stomach.

"He'll be alright, just be on your best behavior okay, Challi, and no talking," Odin replied, his tone firm but gentle. He understood Challi's worries; the world outside was unpredictable, and the road to Fort Lever was fraught with its own dangers. Odin placed a reassuring hand on Challi's shoulder, the solid weight of it grounding both of them in the moment.

As they approached the saloon, Challi and Dusty scanned the dusty street, noting the four or five horses tied up at the rail post. The sun cast long shadows across the ground, and the air was thick with the scent of leather and sweat. Odin stepped up onto the rail boardwalk with a determined stride. He reached for the door of the local saloon, its wooden frame worn from years of use. With a firm push, he swung it open and strode inside, the creak of the floorboards beneath him echoing like a distant thunder.

Challi and Dusty followed closely, their eyes adjusting to the dim light of the saloon. The atmosphere shifted as they entered; the patrons, a mix of weary travelers and hardened locals, paused mid-conversation. Dusty felt the weight of their gazes, curious and perhaps a little judgmental. Odin didn't seem to notice; he had one goal in mind—getting to the bar. He walked toward it, his boots clattering against the wooden floor, a sound that demanded attention.

The bar itself was a polished slab of mahogany, gleaming under the flickering coal oil lamp. Behind it stood a burly bartender, his arms crossed and a faint smirk playing on his lips. A couple of patrons drinking at the bar moved over. Odin stepped up and tapped his finger on the bar and asked for the bartender to bring him three bottles of whiskey. Course he was willing to pay for it. A huge, rough-looking bartender stops Odin in his tracks and looked down at Challi and Dusty.

The raucous laughter of cowboys echoed off the wooden walls, their hats tipped low over sunburnt faces. He felt out of place. As he approached the bar, the bartender's sharp words sliced through the jovial atmosphere. "Can't you read? I don't serve their kind here!"

Odin blinked in confusion, still adjusting to the harshness of the region. His eyes darted to the board mounted on the wall, the white letters stark against the weathered wood: "No Injuns and no dogs allowed!" The message felt like a punch to the gut, the implications sinking in like a stone. He had heard tales of discrimination, but to see it so brazenly displayed in a place he had hoped would welcome him was jarring. The raucous laughter faded into a low murmur, and all eyes turned toward him, the tension palpable.

The cowboys at the bar exchanged glances, their expressions a mix of amusement and contempt. Cowboy 1, a burly figure with a thick mustache, leaned over to his companion, Cowboy 2, and snickered, "Looks like we got ourselves a lost little bird."

Odin stood at the bar, his brow furrowing as he looked down at his coyote, who lay patiently at his feet. The dim light of the saloon flickered casting shadows that danced across the wooden floor. He had just settled in for a drink after a long day, but the bartender's words cut through the air like a gunshot. "Your dog and that Injun boy. They'll have to wait outside. I don't want them here," the bartender barked, wiping the counter with a rag that had seen better days.

"That's no dog, he's a coyote…" Odin began, his voice steady but laced with frustration. He knew that his companion was far more than just a stray animal; the coyote had been with him through thick and thin, a loyal friend in a world that often turned hostile. But the bartender wasn't interested in reason. He crossed his arms defiantly and glared at the two outsiders.

"I don't care if he's General Custer himself, I want that animal outta here," the bartender insisted, his voice rising above the murmurs of the few patrons who had taken refuge in the saloon. The Injun boy, who had been quietly observing the exchange, shifted awkwardly, his dark eyes reflecting the flickering light. He was used to being on the outskirts, yet he felt a kinship with the coyote, a creature often misunderstood and shunned.

Odin took a deep breath, feeling the weight of the bartender's prejudice pressing down on him. "He's just here for companionship, same as us," he replied, trying to keep his voice calm. "We mean no trouble." The coyote, sensing its owner's distress, lifted its head slightly, ears perked, as if to communicate its own plea for acceptance. But the bartender merely shrugged, his resolve unyielding.

Taking a deep breath, Odin straightened his back and met the bartender's gaze. "You don't know me," he replied steadily, his voice rising above the murmurs. "I'm here for three bottles of whiskey." The bar fell silent, the tension hanging in the air like a thundercloud. The bartender's eyes narrowed, but something flickered behind his hardened exterior—a hint of curiosity, perhaps.

The atmosphere shifted, the sharp edges of hostility softening just a fraction. Odin took a step closer, igniting a spark of defiance in the hearts of those who had witnessed his stand. "You can choose to keep this place closed off, or you can open your doors to something new. I'm not here to fight." With that, he turned to the cowboys, his voice steady. "What do you say we share a drink and a story? You might find we're not so different after all." The saloon, once echoing with derision, now buzzed with a hesitant energy, a flicker of hope igniting in the hearts of those present.

The dim light of the bar flickered ominously as Odin leaned against the counter, his eyes scanning the room with an intensity that could slice through steel. Challi stood nearby, his posture relaxed but alert, as if sensing a storm brewing just beneath the surface of the evening. The bartender shuffled nervously behind the counter, glancing at the hidden shotgun beneath the polished wood. It was a familiar scene in this part of town, where tension simmered like a pot on the verge of boiling over.

Suddenly, Odin reached out and patted Challi on the shoulder, a signal that something was about to change. In a swift motion, Odin's hand shot out, disarming the bartender with a flick of his wrist that sent the shotgun clattering to the floor. Dusty began to bark furiously as the bartender's eyes widened in shock, but before he could react, Odin seized him by the shirt, pulling him close. "You think you're tough?" Odin growled, his voice low and dangerous. Without waiting for a reply, he slammed the bartender's face into the bar, the wood splintering slightly under the impact.

With each hit, the sound echoed through the bar like thunder, and blood began to trickle from the bartender's nose, pooling on the surface of the counter. The patrons, who had once been engaged in their own conversations, now stared in disbelief, the atmosphere thick with a mix of fear and anticipation. Odin's savage determination fueled the chaos, and with one final, bone-crushing slam, he released the bartender, who crumpled onto the floor, dazed and bleeding.

With a sudden burst of energy, Dusty leaped onto the bar, startling a few patrons mid-sip. He growled low and fierce, his playful demeanor masking the seriousness of his performance. The saloon fell silent, all eyes on the scrappy pup. Dusty's growls morphed into a series of barks.

"Now I want three bottles of whiskey," Odin declared. Challi stood by, a slight grin creeping onto his face, relishing the power dynamic that had shifted so suddenly. The bartender, groaning and struggling to regain his senses, looked up at Odin with a mix of fear and begrudging respect. In this world, respect could often be purchased with violence, and Odin had just made a very expensive transaction.

The air was thick with the scent of spilled beer and stale smoke. Odin leaned over the counter, his patience wearing thin. The bartender, whose name was lost to both time and regret, swayed precariously as he attempted to comprehend Odin's request. His nose, crimson and swollen from too many encounters with Odin's temper, highlighted the chaotic nature of the evening.

"I said three bottles, not two!" Odin's voice boomed, laced with irritation. With a swift jab, he nose-punched the bartender again, who staggered back, the bottles slipping from his grasp. They clattered to the floor, a symphony of glass breaking against the wood. The bartender barely managed to recover, reaching down beneath the counter where the shadows danced like forgotten spirits. He fumbled through the clutter, his hands trembling as he sought the elusive third bottle, a glimmering promise of whiskey that could soothe the tempest within Odin.

"Here!" the bartender finally shouted, pulling out a dusty bottle that had seen better days. It was a relic of a bygone era. Odin's eyes narrowed, assessing the bartender's choice with skepticism. "You think I want that swill?" he growled, irritation boiling over. The bartender, realizing his mistake, gulped audibly, wishing he could disappear into the shadows. The atmosphere crackled with tension, the other patrons stealing glances, their conversations hushed, as if they were witnesses to a brewing storm. Dusty continued barking furiously.

With a resigned sigh, the bartender retrieved another bottle, this one glistening under the dim coal oil lamp. As he handed it over, he muttered, "Don't hit me again." Odin smirked, the tension easing just a fraction. "I might just let you live," he replied, taking the bottles in one hand and tossing a few coins onto the counter with the other. The bartender watched, a mixture of relief and dread swirling within him, as Odin and Challi sauntered away, a king surveying his domain, leaving chaos in his wake. Dusty jumped down from the bar and onto the sawdust floor and followed them out.

Realizing the futility of the argument, Odin turned to the Injun boy. "Let's step outside," he said softly, knowing that sometimes it was better to walk away than to fight a losing battle. As they exited the saloon, the coyote followed closely, its tail swaying gently behind it. Outside, under the vast expanse of the starry sky, Odin felt a sense of freedom, as if the world beyond those four walls was theirs to explore.

Challi clutched Odin's arm tightly as the rumble of thunder echoed above them. The sky was a deep gray, swirling ominously, and each clap sent a shiver through his spine. They were making their way to Doc Barry's medical office to pick up Jolly. Dusty, trailing behind, flicked his ears nervously at the sound, his eyes wide and alert. Odin tried to reassure them both. "Easy boys, it's just thunder, take it easy," he said, his voice calm amidst the storm.

As they continued down the dirt rocky road, the wind picked up, swirling leaves into a mini tornado around their feet. Challi spoke softly in Sioux, his words barely audible over the increasing roar of the storm. He wished for sunshine, for the warmth that usually filled their days. But today, it seemed the sky had other plans. Dusty pressed closer to Challi, seeking comfort. The trio moved purposefully, each step echoing the urgency of their mission.

Upon reaching Doc Barry's office, they found the door ajar, creaking softly with the gusts of wind. Inside, the familiar smell of antiseptic and herbs greeted them, but it was overshadowed by the sound of a distant rumbling. Doc Barry appeared from the back room, his brow furrowed with concern. "You made it just in time," he said, glancing at the darkening sky. "Jolly's been waiting, but with this storm rolling in, we need to act quickly."

Dark clouds rolled in. The once bright sky had turned a deep gray, and he could feel the first drops of rain splattering against his skin. "What of the horses?" Jolly asked, glancing back at the stable where the animals stood restless, sensing the impending storm. Their soft whinnies echoed in the air, a chorus of unease that mirrored Jolly's own concerns.

"They'll fend for themselves," said Odin, his tone dismissive. He had always been pragmatic, focused on survival and the tasks at hand. The horses, after all, were tough creatures, bred to withstand the elements. But Jolly couldn't shake the worry gnawing at him; they were not just livestock but companions who relied on him for care and protection. As the rain began to pour, turning the dirt rocky road to mud and splattering against the stable's wooden walls, Jolly felt a pang of guilt.

Odin turned away, already heading towards the medial office, his mind elsewhere. Jolly hesitated, feeling the weight of the decision pressing down on him. He knew Odin was right in many respects—animals had instincts, and they could find shelter if needed.

Yet, as thunder rumbled overhead and the wind whipped through the trees, he couldn't help but think of the horses huddled together, frightened by the storm. Without a second thought, he dashed back towards the stable, determined to make sure they were safe.

As he reached the stable, the downpour intensified. Jolly swung open the doors, the scent of damp hay filling his lungs. The horses were there, their eyes wide with fear. He quickly moved to them, soothing them with gentle words and soft strokes as he led them to the back of the stable where they would be protected from the worst of the storm. The rain lashed against the roof, creating a rhythm that calmed his racing heart. Jolly realized that this was more than just a responsibility; it was a bond.

When he finally stepped back outside, the storm was at its peak. Odin, watching from the porch, raised an eyebrow but said nothing. In that moment, Jolly understood that sometimes, it was worth defying practicality for the sake of compassion. The horses would be okay, but more importantly, he had chosen to stand by them, just as they had stood by him through countless seasons.

The thunder clapped again, louder this time, rattling the windows. Challi felt a pang of worry for Jolly, but Odin's steady hand on his shoulder reminded him to stay strong. "Let's get in there," Odin urged, leading the way. With a shared glance of determination, they stepped into the office, ready to face whatever challenges lay ahead, storm or not. The bond between them forged even stronger in the face of nature's wrath, they knew they could weather any storm together.

The whorehouse, known locally as *The Stilted Haven*, stood resiliently above the floodplain, its wooden stilts a testament to years of harsh weather. Whenever storms threatened the town, the locals would gather in its embrace, seeking refuge from the pelting rain and howling winds. On one particular stormy night, Mabel, a spirited woman with laughter that echoed like church bells, stood at the entrance, welcoming the townspeople with a warm smile, despite the tempest raging outside.

Getting tired of watching the horses. Jolly ran out of the stables and headed for the whorehouse where he lumbered in with a thick blanket draped over his shoulders, shaking off droplets of water that had soaked through his cap. He settled into a corner booth, Sister Agnes, the town's kind-hearted nun, arrived, her face flushed from the cold.

She carried with her a basket filled with warm bread, a gesture of comfort that always seemed to brighten the room. Tommy followed closely behind, his mischief evident in his wide grin as he playfully ducked under the low beams.

As the storm howled outside, lashing rain against the windows and rattling the doors of the small town, the tavern glowed like a beacon of warmth and cheer. Inside, Mabel bustled about, pouring drinks and serving up generous slices of her famous freshly baked bread. The aroma filled the room, mingling with laughter and the sound of lively chatter. The townspeople, gathered together for shelter from the tempest, shared stories of days gone by, their voices rising and falling in a comforting rhythm against the backdrop of nature's fury.

In the corner, Jolly with a hearty laugh, had claimed the attention of two lively women. With his arms around them, he regaled the crowd with tales of the last great storm that had nearly swept him away. His voice boomed with enthusiasm as he painted vivid pictures of raging waters and desperate rescues, each embellishment drawing chuckles from his audience. The townspeople leaned in closer, captivated not only by the story but by the infectious spirit of camaraderie that filled the room.

Mabel paused for a moment, her hands busy but her heart full as she watched the scene unfold. She loved these moments when the community came together, the bonds of friendship strengthened by shared experiences and laughter. The storm outside may have raged with unrelenting fury, but within the walls of the whorehouse, there was only warmth and joy. Each clink of glasses and hearty laugh seemed to push back against the darkness that threatened to encroach upon them.

Sister Agnes chimed in with tales of faith and resilience, reminding everyone that they had weathered storms before, both literal and metaphorical. Tommy regaled the crowd with exaggerated accounts of his adventures, drawing laughter and applause from his audience.

As the evening wore on, the storm continued its relentless assault, but inside, the atmosphere transformed into one of celebration. The stories flowed as freely as the drinks, and Mabel found herself joining in, sharing a tale of her own about a summer long ago when the river had swelled beyond its banks. The townspeople laughed and gasped, their imaginations ignited by the tales of adventure and mischief.

Hours passed in the cozy whorehouse, where the storm became a distant memory, overshadowed by the bond of community. As the winds began to die down and the rain lessened to a drizzle, the townspeople felt a sense of unity and strength. They realized that *The Stilted Haven* was more than just a shelter from the storm; it was a gathering place where they could come together, share their lives, and find solace in one another. As they prepared to leave, Mabel looked around, her heart swelling with gratitude for the connections forged, solidifying the belief that no storm could ever break their spirit.

Jolly sat hunched over the bar, the flickering candlelight casting shadows across his wrinkled face. His mind was clouded with the haze of cheap whiskey, and his thoughts drifted in and out of coherence. "How about a poke, little lady?" he slurred, gesturing towards the two women seated nearby. The one with the bright red hair, Madeline, burst into laughter, her eyes sparkling with mischief. The other, Sally, merely shook her head, a look of disdain crossing her features. To them, Jolly was little more than a relic.

"I'll pay ya good," Jolly continued, undeterred by their mockery. His grin was crooked, revealing a few missing teeth and a wealth of confidence that belied his age. But just as the words left his lips, a voice echoed through the dimly lit whorehouse, firm and commanding. "That won't be necessary." The atmosphere shifted as both women turned to see the imposing figure of Odin, Jolly's old partner. He loomed in the doorway, backlit by the faint light from outside, his presence demanding attention.

The laughter died down immediately, replaced by an uneasy tension as Sally and Madeline quickly gathered their belongings and scurried past Odin, their laughter evaporating like mist in the morning sun. Jolly squinted through the haze of inebriation, trying to focus on the familiar silhouette that had once shared countless adventures with him. "Odin?" he croaked, bewildered. The man who had stood by him through thick and thin had become a ghost of sorts, only appearing now when he was most vulnerable.

"Jolly, you old sow," Odin replied, his voice softening as he approached. "What have you gotten yourself into this time?" Jolly could see the concern in Odin's eyes, a stark contrast to the raucous laughter that had filled the room moments before. He felt a pang of guilt wash over him, as the reality of his situation settled in like a thick fog.

Here he was, a has-been in a whorehouse, clinging to memories of a wilder past, while his old friend stood before him, a reminder of who he once was.

With a shaky breath, Jolly straightened himself, trying to regain some semblance of dignity. "Just having a bit of fun, you know?" he said, though the weight of his words felt heavy. Odin shook his head, a hint of a smile playing at the corners of his mouth. "Let's get out of here, my friend. There's still some life left in you yet." Together along with Challi, they stepped into the night, leaving the whorehouse, as the stars above twinkled with the promise of new beginnings.

****

Jolly, Odin, Challi, and Dusty were riding along the trail, their spirits high as they made their way toward Fort Lever. The sun hung brightly in the sky, casting a warm glow over the landscape. The canyon around them was alive with vibrant flora and fauna; wildflowers dotted the ground, and the distant sound of birds chirping filled the air. Each of them was lost in thought, taking in the beauty that surrounded them, their horses trotting steadily along the well-worn path.

As they journeyed, the group marveled at the view stretching out before them. The canyon opened up to reveal miles of creek bottoms, where water danced over rocks and glimmered in the sunlight. Rolling hills rose and fell in the distance, their slopes painted with shades of green and gold. Challi pointed excitedly toward a cluster of pothole duck ponds that sparkled like jewels scattered across the landscape, while Dusty's keen eye caught sight of a herd of deer grazing peacefully in a nearby field.

The smell of fresh earth and blooming flowers filled their lungs, invigorating their spirits as they continued their ride. Odin, with a sense of adventure, suggested a quick detour to explore the rich agriculture fields that lay just beyond the canyon's edge. The others readily agreed, eager to see the crops swaying in the breeze. They steered their horses off the trail, laughter echoing between them as they ventured into the open fields, where the golden grains danced like waves under the sun.

As they approached the border of the fields, Jolly spotted an old barn, weathered but still standing strong. Its red paint had faded over the years, but it held stories of the past within its walls. The friends dismounted and wandered closer, curiosity piqued.

Inside, they found relics of farm life—rusty tools, forgotten hay bales, and the sweet scent of aged wood. It was a glimpse into a world that had thrived long before their time, reminding them of the simple joys of life in the countryside.

With the sun beginning to dip low on the horizon, they decided it was time to resume their journey to Fort Lever. As they mounted their horses once more, they exchanged stories and laughter, their hearts full from the day's adventures. The road ahead beckoned, promising more wonders and memories yet to come, and they rode on, united in their friendship and the beauty of the world around them.

In the heart of the countryside, Jolly remembered owning a sprawling stretch of land that hugged the banks of a winding creek, encompassing nearly four miles of lush habitat. It was known as one of the best spots for

Whitetail deer, boasting a remarkable population that had drawn attention from hunters far and wide. Year after year, Boone and Crockett deer emerged from the thickets, their majestic antlers catching the golden rays of the sun, leaving many a hunter breathless with awe. Jolly took pride in his land, nurturing it to ensure that the deer thrived, and the local ecosystem flourished.

Every autumn, as the leaves turned to fiery hues and the air grew crisp, Jolly transformed his property into a hunting paradise. Odin would help organize the seasonal festivities, welcoming both seasoned hunters and eager novices to experience the thrill of the chase. Challi with dreams of becoming a skilled marksman, his eyes gleaming with excitement at the prospect of tracking the elusive deer. He was captivated not only by the hunt but also by the camaraderie that enveloped the group during their adventures.

As the days passed, the main event of the season approached: the famed Ring Neck Pheasant hunt. This annual tradition attracted enthusiasts from around the globe, all yearning to hear the cackle of the rooster bursting from the underbrush. Odin with a knack for finding the best spots. With his trusty coyote Dusty, by his side, he led the way through the fields, weaving tales of past hunts and the majestic birds that had graced their land. The anticipation built as the group set out, their spirits high, eager for the exhilarating flush that awaited them.

On the day of the hunt, the air was alive with the sounds of nature—the rustle of leaves, the distant calls of birds, and the laughter of friends. As they ventured deeper into the thicket, Jolly recalled the many seasons that had come and gone, each one weaving a tapestry of memories. With every flush of a rooster, the thrill of the hunt surged through them, uniting them in a shared pursuit of adventure. Together, they reveled in the beauty of the land, the challenge of the hunt, and the bonds forged amidst the towering trees and winding creek.

The landscape was a patchwork of shelter belts, where tall trees formed natural windbreaks, and strip fields stretched out under the sun, their rows neatly aligned. Each morning, Odin and his friends would rise before dawn, the air crisp and filled with the promise of a new day, as they planned their tasks around the creek bottoms that meandered through the land.

They stumbled upon a hidden grove nestled between the creek and a dense thicket. It was a magical place, untouched by time, where the trees formed a natural canopy, and the ground was carpeted with vibrant mushrooms and wildflowers. As the fields lay still under a blanket of snow, and the trio found themselves reflecting on the year gone by.

Challi stood at the top of the hill, his heart swelling as he watched the sun dip below the horizon, painting the sky in hues of orange and pink. The fields stretched out before him, a patchwork of greens and yellows, whispering secrets in the gentle breeze. It was a quiet morning, the kind that seemed to promise adventure. With the last rays of sunlight warming his face, he felt a deep connection to the world around him. Each moment was precious, a memory waiting to be woven into the tapestry of her life.

After soaking in the beauty of the sunset, Challi made his way down to the river, the water glistening like a thousand tiny stars scattered across its surface. Armed with his bow and arrow, he settled in, ready to chase after the elusive Walleyes. The thrill of the catch excited him, but it was the tranquility of the river that truly captivated him. The soft lapping of the water against the shore and the occasional call of a distant bird created a symphony of serenity, wrapping around her like a comforting blanket.

Granite rock massive outcropping that had stood sentinel for centuries, loomed nearby. Challi often spoke to Dusty, sharing his thoughts and dreams. He'd tell him about his day, the Walleyes he hoped to catch, and the sunsets he adored. In his mind, Dusty was not just a coyote but a steadfast friend, one who would never judge him and always listen. He imagined him chuckling softly as he recounted his fishing and hunting tales, his presence grounding him in the ever-changing world around them.

Odin and Jolly stood in the dim light of the forest, the rustling leaves whispering secrets of the wild around them. Jolly scratched his head in confusion, "What are we gonna do with him? Uh, I mean you can't turn him over to the authorities at Fort Lever. They likely stick him on a reservation somewheres and he'll never see his kin again."

Odin frowned, his brow furrowed in thought. "I ain't planning on turning him over to the authorities," he said firmly. "I told you I'm heading for the fort to alert them of the Grim brothers. After that, we'll take him to his kin." Odin felt a surge of determination; he would not let this child be lost to the world.

As the sun finally slipped away, casting a twilight spell over the landscape, Challi used his arrow as a spear one last time, a small Walleye shimmering at the end. He laughed, the sound echoing in the stillness, a joyous note in the evening air. Every moment spent here, from the vibrant sunsets to the peaceful fishing, became a cherished memory, a story waiting to be told. With a heart full of gratitude, he promised himself to return to this special place, where the sky kissed the earth, and where friendships, even with a coyote, were forged in the quiet beauty of nature.

As they made their way through the thick underbrush, the forest seemed to come alive around them. Jolly kept glancing back at Challi, who rode silently on his mare mule between them. "What if the Grim brothers find us first? Not likely to forget us," Jolly said, a touch of worry creeping into his voice. Odin shook his head. "We've got to be quick and quiet. We'll get to the fort before they even know we're here."

The journey was tense, filled with the distant sounds of danger lurking just beyond the trees. Every snap of a twig sent the boy flinching, but Odin and Jolly kept their focus. Finally, after what felt like weeks, they reached Fort Lever, its sturdy walls rising against the horizon. Odin took a deep breath, preparing himself to confront the authorities about the Grim brothers and ensure the boy's safety.

Chapter 5

Fort Lever

With the sun setting behind them, they stepped forward, ready to protect the innocent and reunite a family torn apart by fear. Fort Lever stood proud in the rugged embrace of the Dakota Territory, its stone walls a testament to both nature and human ambition. Constructed largely within a cavernous hollow of a sheer cliff face, the fort served as a sanctuary for those who dared venture into the untamed wilderness. Named after Amos Julian Lever, a figure of valor from the Revolutionary War, the fort was a place of strategy and resilience, often echoing with the sounds of drills and the spirited debates of its occupants.

As the days turned into weeks, Fort Lever became a haven for settlers seeking refuge from the unpredictable elements of the Dakota wilderness. News of skirmishes with Native tribes reached their ears, but under Colonel Newt David Lenox's command, the fort remained steadfast, prepared for any eventuality. Training exercises were held daily, and the camaraderie among the soldiers grew stronger as they faced challenges together. The fort became a symbol of hope and determination, standing resolute against the encroaching chaos of the frontier.

The sun was beginning to dip below the horizon, casting long shadows across the rocky stone road of the fortress. Odin and his friends, Jolly and Challi along with Dusty, approached the gates on their horses, the sound of hoofbeats echoing in the quiet evening. They slowed to a halt as they reached the guard tower, its stone walls looming above them. Jolly, riding his spirited Shawnee, leaned forward in his saddle, his eyes scanning the tower for a familiar face.

"I say, Private Longhurst, is the colonel in?" Jolly called out, his voice carrying with the evening breeze. The question hung in the air, mingling with the distant sounds of the fort winding down for the night. Private Longhurst, perched atop the guard tower, turned at the sound of his name. As he peered over the edge, he recognized his friend Jolly and the group of riders gathered below. A smile broke across his face, momentarily easing the monotony of his watch.

"Jolly! Good to see you! Who all you got with ya?" Longhurst shouted back, leaning over the edge to get a better view.

"You remember Brannock, don't ya as for the kid, well… that's Challi," said Jolly.

"Don't recall knowing a Brannock. As for the colonel he's inside, but he's busy with reports from the recent skirmish." There was an edge of concern in his voice, a reminder of the ongoing troubles beyond the fortress walls. The camaraderie they shared was a comfort, even in times like these. Odin adjusted his grip on the reins, sensing the tension in the air and the weight of their responsibilities.

"Busy, as always," Odin replied, trying to keep the mood light. "We thought we might catch him for a quick word. Can you let him know we're here?" The group nodded in agreement, wishing for a moment of respite from their burdens. Longhurst, understanding the bond shared among friends, nodded and promised to pass along their message.

As the sun dipped lower, painting the sky in hues of orange and purple, Odin and his friends waited patiently at the gate, their hearts tied to the fortress. The night crept in, but their spirits remained high, united by friendship and the hope of brighter days ahead.

Odin took a deep breath, glancing at the sky as clouds began to gather ominously overhead. "Take your time, son," squawked Odin.

"Don't pay no mind to Brannock, he's just a sour old thing," said Jolly, the ever-optimistic companion. Jolly, with his bright smile and jovial demeanor, was the kind of person who could lighten the mood even on the grimmest of days.

Private Longhurst climbed down the wooden ladder from the guard house, his boots clanging softly against the rungs as he descended. The sun hung low in the sky, casting long shadows across the fort's courtyard. As he reached the ground, he straightened his uniform and approached Colonel Lenox, who stood with his arms crossed, deep in thought. "Colonel," Longhurst began, his voice steady, "Jolly wants a word with you."

Colonel Lenox, a man of few words but great authority, nodded curtly. He waved his hand dismissively, a signal for Longhurst to proceed with the message. The colonel's demeanor was stern, yet there was an air of anticipation that hung between them. Longhurst saluted sharply, the crisp sound echoing in the stillness, and then turned to walk back out of the command office.

As he marched up the ladder, Longhurst felt the familiar rush of duty surge through him. Each rung brought him closer to his post at the top of the fort, where he could see the expanse of the territory beyond. He reached the top and paused for a moment, with a wave of his hand, the private beckoned Jolly and the others rode in, feeling a sense of camaraderie that only those in service could understand.

They reached the command office. Odin was the first to pull back on his reins as did Jolly and Challi. Odin and Jolly stepped down from their horses only Challi stayed put on his mare mule and was told that they would be back in a jiffy. Odin and Jolly approached with a purposeful stride, their expression a mix of determination and urgency. Longhurst stepped aside to let them through the heavy wooden door that led into the command office.

As they entered, the atmosphere shifted; the air was thick with the weight of unspoken words and the responsibility that lay ahead. Longhurst took his position by the door, ready to assist in whatever capacity was needed, while the conversation between Jolly, Odin and Colonel Lenox began, a meeting of minds destined to shape the fate of the fort and its men.

Colonel Lenox leaned back in his creaking chair, the dim light of the oil lamp casting shadows across his weathered face. The air in the makeshift office was thick with tension as Odin stood across from him, his fists clenched at his sides. "What can I do for you?" the colonel asked, his tone betraying a hint of weariness. Odin's eyes burned with anger as he recounted the horrors he had witnessed near Snakefist's village, the charred remains of homes, and the gruesome sight of bodies strewn across the ground. "You can start by searching for the Grim brothers, theirs about seven of them scalp hunters," he demanded, his voice rising. "They're in the area, scalping Sioux braves, women, and even children."

The Colonel's expression hardened, and he began to respond, "Nothing. There's nothing the law or me for that matters that says scalping is against the law…" His words hung in the air, heavy with the weight of indifference. Jolly stepped forward, his brow furrowed in disbelief.

"That's horse shit and you know it, Colonel. So, you're gonna let the Grim brothers do whatever they damn well please, all because it's not against the law?" The tension crackled like the dry prairie grass outside, and the colonel could feel the pressure building, the looming threat of violence hanging over the conversation.

As the words echoed in the small room, the Colonel's mind raced. He knew the Grim brothers, notorious for their ruthless ways, were a law unto themselves. The thought of them roaming free, committing unspeakable acts against the Sioux, made his stomach churn. "What do you expect me to do?" he asked, his voice low, betraying a flicker of uncertainty. "I'm just one man, and the law doesn't seem to care." Odin stepped closer, the fire in his gaze igniting a flicker of resolve within the Colonel. "You can start by standing up for what's right, Colonel. Even if it means going against the law."

In that moment, the colonel felt a shift within himself. The weight of duty pressed down on him, forcing him to confront the truth of his own complicity. He couldn't turn a blind eye to the atrocities being committed against the Sioux people any longer. "Alright," he said finally, a newfound determination settling in his chest. "I'll do what I can to put a stop to this. But I'll need your help." Odin nodded, a glimmer of hope igniting in his heart, while Jolly crossed his arms, a look of approval on his face. Together, they would confront the Grim brothers and seek justice for those who had suffered, stepping into the unknown with the courage of men who knew the cost of silence.

Meanwhile, Challi still sitting on his mare mule, his throat parched from the relentless sun beating down on him. They'd been traveling for days through the endless brush, but the only thing he had found was a worn-out supply box that held three bottles of whiskey. He had heard tales of this drink back in the village, stories told by the old folks in the saloon, where laughter and raucous voices echoed against the wooden walls. But Challi had never tasted it himself, and curiosity gnawed at him. What was it about whiskey that made the white-eyed folks hang around saloons, losing themselves in its embrace?

Feeling the weight of his thirst, Challi glanced around to make sure no one was watching. He carefully lifted one of the bottles from the box, its glass cool and inviting against his palm. With a swift motion, he unscrewed the cap and took a deep breath, the sharp scent of alcohol filling his nostrils. He hesitated for a moment, thoughts racing through his mind. What would Odin think?

He always warned him about the dangers of drinking, how it could twist the mind and lead to foolishness. But the thirst was overpowering, and with a determined nod, he brought the bottle to his lips.

The liquid slid down his throat like fire, burning yet exhilarating. Challi coughed and spluttered, surprised by the intensity of the taste. But as he continued to drink, the warmth spread through him, loosening the tight knots of worry and fatigue. Laughter bubbled up from deep within, an unexpected joy that he had seldom felt in the harshness of life. He began to sway, the world around him spinning in a colorful blur, and for the first time, he felt free—free from thirst, free from responsibility, free from the burden of survival.

As Odin and Jolly appeared out on the command office's porch, they all heard a *thud*. Jolly witnessed Challi fall from his mare mule onto the hard ground. "What have you done, boy?" he chuckled, his voice gravelly with age, yet laced with a hint of amusement. Challi could only grin, his thoughts a chaotic jumble, feeling like a king in a realm of laughter. Speaking in Sioux, his words slurring together. Jolly shook his head, a smirk dancing on his lips. He had seen many a young soul succumb to the allure of spirits and knew the dangers lurking behind the haze of drunkenness.

As the sun dipped below the horizon, painting the sky in hues of orange and purple, Challi found himself sprawled on the ground, the world still spinning. Odin's worried face flashed in his mind, and for a fleeting moment, he felt a pang of regret. But the warmth of the whiskey wrapped around him like a comforting blanket, and he surrendered to the chaos. He laughed at the stars beginning to twinkle above, unaware of the lessons that awaited him in the morning light. In that moment, all that mattered was the joy of the now, the intoxicating freedom that came with a bottle and a heart unburdened.

It was a sight that stirred a mix of concern and amusement in Odin. "You really should slow down, Challi," he said, trying to maintain a tone of seriousness midst the revelry. But Challi merely waved a dismissive hand, his cheeks flushed with the warmth of the drink.

Jolly chimed in. "Taint nothing wrong with putting a little hair on your chest! I took a swig when I was his age," he proclaimed, slapping Challi on the back with enough force to nearly topple him over. Odin couldn't shake the feeling that someone needed to be the voice of reason.

Colonel Lenox started to laugh heartily at Jolly's comment. "But you also ended up with more than just hair, didn't you, Jolly?" he retorted, a twinkle of jest in his eye. But Odin felt the weight of the night pressing down on him, the reckless abandon of his friends contrasting sharply with the serious matters that loomed outside the fort walls.

As the evening wore on, Odin found himself caught between the light-hearted banter and the gravity of their lives. Challi let out a loud guffaw, and Odin couldn't help but smile, even as he worried about the dangers that lay just beyond the horizon. Perhaps it was good for them to unwind, to momentarily forget the burdens they carried.

Colonel Lenox stood with his arms crossed, glaring at Odin. The sun hung low in the sky, casting long shadows over the ground. "Mr. Brannock, you didn't tell me that you brought a Sioux boy on post. I'm gonna have to ask you to turn him over to me," he said, his voice firm and commanding. Beside him, Jolly shifted uncomfortably, glancing at the young boy who stood nervously by his side, who was still a tad drunk.

"Yep, see I told ya, Odin," Jolly murmured, trying to lighten the tension. But Odin with wide, scared eyes, held his ground. "No, sir, I'll not turn him over," he declared, his tone steady despite the fear that flickered in his gaze. He had grown fond of the boy, who had been traveling with them since the terrible events that led him to escape his home.

Colonel Lenox's expression hardened. "But Mr. Brannock, you must. He's a Sioux refugee and must be returned to his people on the reservation," he insisted, the authority in his voice echoing against the wooden walls of the post. The colonel believed he was doing the right thing, enforcing the rules that he felt were necessary to maintain order.

"What people? He has none. The scalp hunters saw to that," Odin replied, his voice low but filled with conviction. The weight of his words hung in the air. The boy had lost everything, and now he was lost in a world that felt both strange and unwelcoming. Odin placed a reassuring hand on Challi's shoulder, silently promising that he would not let him go back to the pain he once knew.

The tension between the men thickened like fog, each unwilling to back down. In that moment, the boy's future hung in the balance, a fragile thread woven between duty and compassion. As the sun dipped below the horizon, casting a golden glow over the post, the weight of their choices loomed larger than ever. Would they choose to follow the rules, or would they dare to rewrite them for the sake of a boy who had already lost so much?

The sun setting behind Colonel Lenox, casting long shadows over the dry earth. With a confident demeanor, he approached Challi, who stood rooted to the spot, his face a mask of uncertainty. "The Lakota people would be glad to take him in," Lenox said, gesturing toward the horizon where the tribes lived, their traditions rich and vibrant against the backdrop of the wilderness. But Challi shook his head vehemently, as if the very spell that once filled him with hope had vanished into thin air.

Jolly chuckled lightly, his eyes sparkling with mischief. "Well, that settles that don't it? He's traveling with us," he remarked, his voice tinged with amusement, as if the decision were just another light-hearted banter among friends. The implications of Challi's reluctance hung heavy in the air, yet Jolly seemed unfazed, as he often did when faced with the seriousness of the world.

Colonel Lenox, however, was not one to back down easily. "You can't be serious?" he pressed, his brow furrowing with concern. "There are people who would welcome you, Challi. You could find a new home among them." But Challi felt an invisible tether pulling him back, a connection to the land he knew and loved, one that could not be severed by the promise of safety or acceptance elsewhere.

As the sun dipped below the horizon, casting a brilliant array of colors across the sky, Challi took a deep breath, the scent of earth and sage filling his lungs. He felt the weight of the decision before him, a choice between two worlds. Challi spoke in Sioux stating that he was going with Odin and Jolly.

Lenox and Jolly exchanged glances, realizing that sometimes, the greatest journeys do not take one away but rather anchor them deeper into their roots. In that moment, they understood Challi's conviction, realizing that the true magic lay not in the allure of new beginnings but in the strength of one's heritage—a truth as profound as the endless sky above them.

Under the pale light of the moon, Hadly Proctor and his three companions emerged from the shadows of the hill, their rifles gleaming like stars against the darkened sky. Clad in buffalo hides, they moved with a purpose that sent an eerie chill through the night air. Dusty who had been with Odin through thick and thin, instinctively flattened his ears against his head, sensing the palpable tension that hung in the atmosphere. Odin stood resolute, his eyes locked on Proctor, heart racing with courage. He had faced many challenges, but this felt different—more sinister.

As Proctor's steely gaze settled on them, the forest around them seemed to hold its breath, the usual sounds of the night replaced by an unsettling silence. The only noise was the occasional rustle of leaves stirred by a gentle breeze and the distant howl of a wolf, a reminder of the wildness that surrounded them. Dusty's instincts kicked in, urging him to protect his friend at all costs. Odin could feel the weight of the moment pressing down on him, the bond between him and Dusty stronger than ever as they braced themselves for the confrontation ahead.

The night air was cool, as the troopers lit a fire in the middle of the parade ground the flickering flames cast dancing shadows on the faces of the men. Challi whispered to Dusty in his native language, a sound that was both soothing and mysterious. Odin shifted uncomfortably, his gaze fixed on the colonel as he tried to decipher the tension in the air.

"Do you know Proctor?" Lenox asked, breaking the silence and turning his attention to Odin. The question hung heavily, as if it held secrets waiting to be uncovered. Odin shook his head slowly, unsure of what to make of the colonel or the implications of his words. Dusty, standing close to Challi, exchanged glances with the boy, a silent understanding passing between them.

The night was thick with uncertainty, and they could feel the weight of the Colonel's authority.

"Relax, Mr. Brannock," Lenox continued, his voice steady and reassuring. "He and the others are from a scouting party. I sent out early looking for renegade Indians." His words did little to ease the tension that clung to the air, but there was a certain confidence in his demeanor. "I'll see to them," he added, glancing at Jolly and then back at Odin. "You, Jolly, and the Indian boy must stay overnight, and we'll talk more about your current situation in the morning."

As the fire crackled and popped, the group settled into an uneasy quiet. Challi noticed the way Odin's brow furrowed, the newcomer clearly grappling with the unknowns of their mission. Dusty, sensing the boy's unease, walked over toward him nuzzled his hand to reassure him. Together, they watched as the colonel moved about the parade ground, preparing for the night ahead, while the stars twinkled overhead, indifferent to the worries of the men below. The shadows grew longer, and the night deepened, but within that darkness lay the promise of dawn and the revelations it might bring.

Challi tugged at Jolly's shirt, his small hands gripping the fabric tightly as he tried to get his attention. With wide eyes filled with urgency, he spoke in Sioux, his voice a mix of pleading and frustration. Jolly merely shrugged him off, his mind focused on the matter at hands. Odin, leaning against an old oak tree, was too engrossed in his own thoughts to notice Challi's distress.

"Proctor!" Challi shouted, his voice rising above the chatter, pointing a finger at the man who stood confidently at the edge of the gathering. Proctor, with his rugged charm and disarming smile, seemed to radiate an aura of trust. But to Challi, he was a figure shrouded in darkness, a man who had murdered his father. The weight of his words hung heavily in the air, but Jolly and Odin continued to talk, unaware of the storm brewing within Challi's heart.

Desperation clawed at Challi as he repeated his warning, his Sioux words tumbling out in a desperate rush. He tried to convey the truth, the pain of loss that had carved its way into his young soul. Yet, the sounds of commandment drowned him out, and he felt invisible amid the vibrant colors of the celebration. The adults danced, and the children played, while Challi stood alone, a solitary figure against the backdrop of ignorance and indifference.

With a deep breath, Challi realized he needed to show them the truth. He turned to Proctor, who was now laughing with a group of friends, and his heart raced. Summoning every ounce of courage, Challi dashed forward, ready to confront the man who had haunted his dreams. But as he approached, he caught a glimpse of Proctor's face, and in that moment, he knew that the path to Sioux justice would be far more complicated than he had ever imagined.

Chapter 6

Challi's heart raced as he sprinted towards Odin, the weight of his father's death heavy on his shoulders. The cutting knife felt cold in his hand, a chilling reminder of the vengeance he sought. Proctor, the man who had taken everything from him, stood unaware, oblivious to the storm brewing in Challi's heart. With every step, Challi's determination grew; this was not just an act of revenge, it was his way of reclaiming his family's honor. The air crackled with tension as he raised the knife, ready to end Proctor's life.

Jolly, standing nearby, caught sight of Challi's fierce intent and quickly intervened. "Whoa there squirt, what do you think you're doing?" His voice cut through the haze of anger clouding Challi's mind. Jolly knew the cost of such actions, the weight of decisions made in blind fury. Challi's eyes were wild, his thoughts consumed by the image of his father. He spoke in Sioux, words spilling out in a torrent of grief and rage, declaring his desire to avenge the wrongs done to his family.

Odin, sensing the danger in Challi's actions, stepped forward with a calm authority. He addressed Challi in Sioux, his tone soothing yet firm. "What is wrong, Challi? Why do you want to kill Proctor?" Odin sought to understand the turmoil that churned within the young boy, hoping to quell the fire of vengeance that threatened to consume him. The knife trembled in Challi's grip as he grappled with the emotions swirling in his chest, torn between justice and the desperate need for peace.

As the moments ticked by, the world around them faded into silence, all eyes fixed on Challi. The weight of his decision loomed large, and for a brief instant, he faltered. Memories of his father's laughter intertwined with the pain of loss, creating a complex tapestry of love and sorrow. Perhaps vengeance was not the answer; perhaps forgiveness held the key to healing. Challi lowered the knife slightly, uncertainty flickering in his gaze as he began to reconsider the path he was about to take.

"Why is that boy staring at me?" Proctor's voice boomed, cutting through the silence with a sharp edge. Odin, feeling the surge of adrenaline, stepped forward, his own voice steady as he replied, "The boy thinks you murdered his father, did ya? The Sioux seek only to protect this land," The tension crackled in the air, a storm waiting to break. Dusty growled softly, a warning to the intruders, as the three men exchanged glances, assessing the resolve of the duo before them.

Proctor leaned back against the rough-hewn hitching post, his face shadowed under the brim of his weathered hat. "No, I don't take to Indians," he muttered, dismissing the thought with a wave of his hand. A faint breeze stirred the air, carrying the scent of the nearby pines and the hint of something else—tension.

Jolly, always quick with a retort, stepped forward, hands on his hips. "No, you just scalp them," he shot back, a smirk dancing on his lips. Challi, a mere spectator in this exchange, watched with wide eyes. He had seen things that made his heart race, tales that danced on the edge of nightmares, and he wasn't afraid to speak up.

Proctor's brow furrowed, and he turned to Challi, his expression darkening. "You calling me a liar?" The accusation hung in the air, heavy and charged. Jolly stepped closer, sensing the rising tension. "If the shoe fits, the boy seen it happen and I believe him," he declared, his voice steady as he positioned himself between Proctor and the boy, ready to defend the truth that lay in the child's words.

Challi shifted nervously but held his ground. He glanced between the two men, the weight of their words pressing down on him like a storm cloud. Speaking in Sioux, "I saw it," he insisted, recalling the haunting image of the shadows that danced across the campfire that night, the whispers that echoed in the wind. Proctor's mouth tightened, and for a moment, the world around them seemed to pause, the silence heavy with unspoken truths.

"I hate being called a liar, especially from a runt-like Indian brat, who can't back up his story," said Proctor.

Dusty was about to get involved as he growled at Proctor as if to say, "better not touch him,". Dusty was quite fond of the boy and nobody was going to harm him. Least while he was around.

"And I ain't scare of no coyote either, I've skinned me some a few years back," said Proctor.

Odin stood in the dusty parade ground, his brow furrowed in confusion as he watched the spectacle unfold before him. Proctor, towered over Challi, who was much smaller in stature. Proctor had a reputation for pushing around the younger kids, but today, it seemed like he had chosen the wrong target. Challi, with a defiant glint in his eye, stood his ground, refusing to back down. Odin couldn't help but marvel at the scene; it was rare to see someone confront Proctor so boldly.

"Alright, that's enough," Odin called out, his voice steady despite the tension hanging in the air. "We know how you can pick on a little boy. How are you besting against the bigger ones?" His words hung in the air like an unsteady bridge, daring Proctor to cross it. The other kids watched, their eyes wide with anticipation, unsure of how the bully would respond.

Proctor, taken aback by the unexpected support for Challi, hesitated. He was used to intimidation, not being challenged directly. The laughter and jeers from the other men encouraged Challi, who took a small step forward, his fists clenched. Odin felt a surge of pride for his young friend; Challi was no longer just a target. He had become someone who stood up for himself, and that made all the difference.

With the atmosphere charged, Proctor scoffed, trying to regain his composure. "You think you can take me on? He's nothing more than Indian brat!" But there was a crack in his bravado. The group of soldiers surrounding them began to chant Challi's name, their voices rising in unison, fortifying his courage. In that moment, it was clear that the tide was turning; Challi's bravery inspired others to find their voice against the bully.

"I'll remember this boy, and I'll come through the night on tipsy-toes and get ya for sure. And no coyote will save ya either," said Proctor.

In the midst of this standoff, Colonel Lenox appeared behind Proctor, silent yet commanding. Colonel Lenox seemed to exude an aura of power, his intentions cloaked in secrecy. Every instinct in Odin urged him to remain vigilant. As Colonel Lenox stepped forward, the moonlight revealed a face etched with wisdom and weariness, eyes that had seen countless battles.

"There is more at stake here than you realize," Colonel Lenox spoke softly, their voice laced with an ancient knowledge that resonated deep within Odin.

With the fate of their world hanging in the balance, Odin and Dusty stood firm, ready to confront whatever trials lay ahead. The enchanted realm around them pulsed with magic and danger, each heartbeat resonating with the promise of adventure. The bond between the boy and his wolf would be tested like never before, but together, they would face the shadows that threatened to engulf their home. The night was far from over, and the path ahead was fraught with uncertainty, but in that moment, they knew they were not alone.

Proctor glanced around, taking in the sights of troopers, their faces illuminated by the soft glow of camp lights. "Come one, let's leave this party," he said. He felt a restless energy in the atmosphere, a tension brewing beneath the surface that made him uneasy.

Jolly shot Proctor a disapproving look. "You gonna let 'em get away with that? I mean damn, you should have locked them up in the guard house or something," he retorted, his brow furrowed in concern. He gestured toward a group of revelers in the corner who appeared to be getting a little too rowdy, their laughter bordering on chaos. Jolly believed that order was essential, especially in such a public setting.

Colonel Lenox entered the conversation with a dismissive wave of his hand. "There's no reason for that. They're just out having a good time; just let them be," he said, his tone soothing yet firm. He had seen enough of life's ups and downs to know that sometimes, letting loose was just what people needed.

Jolly stood at the edge of Fort Lever, his eyes following Proctor and his men as they mounted their horses, their figures silhouetted against the setting sun. The distant sound of hooves echoed in the silence, a reminder of the mission they had just embarked upon. Jolly felt a mix of anxiety and curiosity swirling within him. "What do we do now? Follow them?" he asked, turning to Odin, who was leaning against the fort's weathered wall.

Odin glanced back at Jolly, his expression calm and collected. "No, let 'em be for the time being," he replied, his voice steady. He had a knack for knowing when to act and when to wait, a skill honed through years on the frontier. Jolly respected Odin's judgment, but the restlessness in his chest urged him to take action. He couldn't shake the feeling that Proctor was up to something that required their attention.

Jolly paced back and forth. "What if they're planning somethin' ? We can't just sit here and do nothing," he insisted, glancing back at the path Proctor had taken. Odin chuckled softly, a sound that seemed to ease Jolly's tension slightly. "Sometimes the best move is to gather information first. We don't know their intentions yet."

With a sigh, Jolly nodded, albeit reluctantly. He admired Odin's wisdom but wished for more direct action. The minutes turned into hours as they stood watch, the night creeping in with its blanket of stars. Eventually, Jolly found a spot to sit, leaning against the fort's sturdy wall. As the night deepened, he realized that waiting could sometimes reveal more than rushing into the unknown. They would see what awaited them at dawn, and perhaps then, they could decide their next move together, ready for whatever Proctor had in store.

****

As the night grew deeper, the stars twinkled like distant lanterns in a vast, dark sea. Challi, unable to find solace in sleep, quietly slipped out of his corner of the command office. He tiptoed over to Odin, who was resting peacefully, and crawled in between Jolly and Dusty, who were nestled comfortably together. With a soft mumble in Sioux, Challi's eyelids grew heavy, and he drifted off into a dreamless slumber, the warmth of his companions wrapping around him like a protective cocoon.

Jolly, feeling the shift in the bed, turned to Odin with a puzzled expression. "What was all that about?" he whispered, trying not to disturb Challi's newfound peace. Odin, still half-asleep, furrowed his brow, contemplating the situation. "I honestly don't know unless…" he began, his voice trailing off as he searched for the right words. The bunkhouse was thick with the quiet anticipation of the night, every creak of the house echoing their thoughts.

"Unless what?" Jolly pressed, curiosity dancing in his eyes. Odin took a moment, still wrapped in the haze of sleep, and finally spoke, "Unless he thinks of us as his father." The weight of the statement hung in the air, wrapping around them like the woolen blanket Odin had pulled over himself. It was a revelation that stirred something deep within them, a realization of the bond they shared with Challi, who had wandered into their lives like a lost star seeking a constellation.

As Challi slept, peaceful dreams took him to faraway lands filled with laughter and light. He felt the warmth of his companions, and in that moment, everything felt right. Odin and Jolly exchanged glances, both silently acknowledging the truth in Odin's words. Dusty, still nestled against Jolly, let out a soft snore, adding to the serenity of the night. Wrapped in their shared warmth, they all drifted closer, united by the unspoken promise of protection and care. In the heart of the night, a family was quietly woven together, their bonds strengthening with each passing moment.

****

The sun peeked over the horizon, casting a warm golden glow across the landscape. Odin and Jolly sprang out of their beds, excitement coursing through their veins. They had been eagerly waiting for this day, the day they would ride into the vast wilderness surrounding Fort Lever. Jolly, with his easy-going nature, turned to their young friend Challi, who was still nestled in the bed, lost in dreams of grand adventures.

"Challi, it's time to ride," Jolly said gently, tapping him on the shoulder with a light touch. His voice was patient yet filled with the thrill of the day ahead. Challi stirred, blinking sleep from his eyes as he slowly adjusted to the morning light. He felt the cool breeze brush against his skin and the scent of pine trees wafting through the air, invigorating him.

With a yawn and a stretch, Challi slowly sat up, his mind still a little foggy from sleep. He remembered the plans they had made the night before, the promise of adventure. He turned to Odin, who was already checking the supplies on Thor, ensuring everything was in order for their ride. In Sioux, he called out to Odin, signaling that he was ready to join them.

Odin looked back, a grin spreading across his face as he replied in kind. The camaraderie between the three friends was palpable, their bond strong as they prepared for the journey ahead. With the sun rising higher, they saddled their horses, excitement bubbling between them. The day was ripe for exploration, and as they set off, the world around them seemed to awaken, ready to share its secrets.

Colonel Lenox stood at the gates of Fort Lever, his silhouette framed against the rising sun that painted the sky in hues of orange and gold. He waved goodbye to Odin and Jolly, who sat tall upon their horses, the animals snorting softly as they felt the tension of the morning air. Challi and Dusty, followed closely behind, their eyes gleaming with anticipation. They all knew that the path ahead would be fraught with challenges, but the promise of the Montana Territory beckoned them like a distant star.

As they rode into the wilderness, the trees whispered secrets of the land, their leaves rustling gently in the breeze. The trail to Red River was narrow and winding, snaking through the underbrush and leading them deeper into the embrace of nature. Jolly took the lead as Odin felt a mix of excitement and apprehension; this journey was not just about reaching a destination, but also about the bonds they would forge and the stories they would create along the way. He glanced back at his companions, their expressions a blend of determination and eagerness, and felt a swell of pride.

With each mile they traveled, the world around them transformed. The sound of hooves on the dirt road became a rhythmic melody, punctuated by the occasional call of a bird or the rustle of a small creature in the bushes. Odin and Jolly shared their knowledge of the land, recounting stories of explorers and pioneers who had come before them, their voices echoing with a sense of history that connected them to the earth beneath their horses.

As the sun climbed higher in the sky, the heat began to shimmer on the horizon. They stopped for a brief rest, allowing the horses to drink from a nearby stream. Odin took a moment to reflect on their journey so far. Each of them brought something unique to this expedition, and he felt confident that together they could overcome whatever obstacles lay ahead. The Montana Territory awaited, filled with promise and opportunity, but it was the camaraderie they shared that would truly make this adventure unforgettable.

With renewed energy, they mounted their horses once more, determination etched on their faces. The wilderness stretched before them, inviting yet unpredictable, and as they resumed their journey, Jolly led the way with a steady resolve. The road to Red River was just the beginning, an open canvas upon which they would paint their tale of friendship, bravery, and the search for a new life in the vast expanse of the frontier.

Odin and Jolly trudged along the rocky path that wound through the dense forest, their shadows stretching long in the late afternoon sun. The air was thick with the scent of damp earth and the chatter of distant birds. Odin glanced over his shoulder. "I don't know about you, Jolly, but I get the sneaking feeling that someone's following us," he said, his voice low and tinged with concern.

Jolly grinned and shrugged off the unease. "How many you reckon?" he asked, twirling a stick he had picked up from the ground. To Jolly, the woods were an adventure, a place where imagination ran wild. But Odin's furrowed brow spoke of a different story—one of caution and the instinctive wariness that comes with age.

"Well, can't rightly say," Odin replied, his eyes narrowing as he scanned the trees that loomed on either side of the path. "Might be just old age creeping upon me." He chuckled softly, attempting to lighten the mood, but the laughter felt hollow against the backdrop of the whispering pines. The feeling of being watched lingered in the air, palpable and unsettling.

They continued riding, the crunch of leaves underfoot amplifying the silence that enveloped them. Each rustle of the branches overhead made Odin's heart race a little faster, while Jolly's laughter echoed through the woods, a stark contrast to his companion's growing sense of dread. He felt the weight of his years, the burden of wisdom that warned him of unseen dangers lurking just beyond their sight.

As they reached a clearing, the sun dipped lower, casting long shadows that danced like phantoms. Jolly paused, looking back at Odin, who stood still, a sentinel in the dimming light. "Maybe it's just a deer or a curious squirrel," Jolly suggested, trying to dismiss the tension. But Odin shook his head, a chill running down his spine. "It's not always what it seems, my friend." And in that moment, the forest held its breath, as if waiting for the truth to reveal itself.

Jolly riding in the middle of the grassy field, the sun shining brightly above, casting playful shadows as he began to whistle a cheerful tune. It was a melody that danced through the air, but it quickly morphed into a cacophony of off-key notes as he broke into song. "Oh, the stars are bright, and the sky is blue, la-la-la, just me and you!" he belted out, his voice wobbling in all the wrong places. Odin frowned deeply, his eyebrows furrowing in irritation.

"How can anyone think whilst you sing, and god-awful I might add at that," Odin retorted, shaking his head as if trying to dislodge the sound from his ears. Jolly merely laughed, undeterred by Odin's criticism. "Aw, shut up! Challi likes it, don't ya?" he called out, glancing at Challi. Challi, with a wide grin, attempted to mimic Jolly's awkward singing, his voice a high-pitched squeak that echoed through the field.

"See! He likes it! Sing along, Challi!" Jolly encouraged, his enthusiasm infectious. Challi, eager to please, opened his mouth wide and let out a series of garbled sounds that resembled a song more than anything coherent. Jolly continued to sing with unabashed glee, his off-key notes mixing with Challi's squeals. The duo created a peculiar harmony that filled the air with laughter, and even Odin couldn't help but crack a small smile despite his best efforts to remain stoic.

As the three of them enjoyed their impromptu concert, the worries of the day began to fade away. The sun dipped lower in the sky, casting a golden glow around them, and for a fleeting moment, the world felt lighter. Odin sighed, realizing that perhaps there was something to this chaos after all. "Alright, fine! Just don't blame me when the birds start flying away in terror," he said, finally relenting. Jolly's grin widened, and Challi clapped his tiny hands, thrilled by the unexpected harmony of friendship that had formed amidst the off-key notes and carefree laughter.

Odin pulled back on Thor's reins, bringing the mighty steed to a sudden stop. The clatter of hooves faded as Jolly and Challi continued to sing their off-key melodies, their voices ringing through the otherwise tranquil forest. Dusty raised his nose to the air, his senses tingling as he caught a whiff of something foul. It was a stench that made his fur bristle and his growl rumble deep within his chest.

Odin, ever vigilant, scanned the terrain with his keen eyes, searching for the source of Dusty's distress. The trees stood tall and silent, the only movement being the gentle sway of leaves in the light breeze. There was no sign of danger, yet Dusty remained resolute, refusing to budge an inch. His instincts were not to be ignored, and Odin understood that something was amiss, even if the forest seemed peaceful.

"Jolly! Challi! Quiet down for a moment," Odin commanded, his voice firm yet calm. The singing halted abruptly, and the two friends exchanged puzzled glances. They turned their attention to Dusty, who continued to sniff the air, his growls growing more intense. Odin dismounted Thor as he approached the coyote. "What is it, boy?" he asked, kneeling beside Dusty.

The coyote's eyes were focused, unwavering, on a thicket of bushes nearby. Odin followed his gaze, a sense of unease creeping into his heart. "Stay close," he instructed Jolly and Challi, who now stood at the ready, their earlier gaiety forgotten. With a deep breath, Odin edged toward the bushes, parting the branches with caution. What lay beyond would either reveal a hidden threat or be nothing more than a trick of the wind. Dusty barked, his loyalty unwavering, as Odin prepared to confront whatever lay ahead, the harmony of their journey hanging in the balance.

Proctor stood at the edge of the valley, his voice cutting through the quiet like a knife. "I told you, Mister, I'll come and get your little brat," he declared, the words heavy with a sinister promise. The sun hung low in the sky, casting long shadows that danced ominously around him. Challi, kicked his mare mule to hide among the thick bushes, felt his heart race. He knew Proctor meant every word, and the threat to the child was all too real.

Odin, ever vigilant, felt the tension in the air shift. Without hesitation, he reached for his Henry rifle, its weight familiar and reassuring in his hands. He had been prepared for this moment, knowing Proctor's reputation as a man who did not shy away from violence. "You'll have to go through me first," he said, his voice steady but low, as he took a position that offered him the best vantage point. The wind rustled the leaves, almost as if nature itself held its breath in anticipation of what was to come.

Challi's mind raced as he considered his options. The valley was vast, and though he felt cornered, he knew he had to protect himself at all costs. He pulled back on his mare mule slid off and crept silently, his eyes never leaving Proctor, who was now scanning the area with a predatory gaze. The tension crackled in the air, thick enough to feel, and Challi's resolve hardened. He would not let fear dictate his actions; he would fight.

As Proctor took a step forward, a glint of sunlight caught the barrel of Odin's rifle. He leveled the weapon, aiming carefully. "You're making a mistake, Proctor," he warned, his finger resting lightly on the trigger. The moment hung heavy, a stillness that seemed to stretch into eternity. Challi felt a surge of hope; perhaps together they could drive Proctor away before he could make good on his threat.

But Proctor simply laughed, a cold, mirthless sound that echoed across the valley. "You think you can stop me?" he taunted, his confidence unwavering. The confrontation was imminent, and as the sun dipped below the horizon, the shadows grew longer, mirroring the darkness of the intentions that loomed ahead. In that moment, Challi and Odin stood united, ready to defend their world against the encroaching storm.

Odin stood resolute, his hand steady on the wooden stock of his Henry rifle, the sun casting sharp shadows on the dusty ground. Proctor's voice echoed in his mind, a sinister promise that stirred the tension thick in the air, "Got three men just itching to pull down on you, Mister." The words hung there like a noose, tightening around Odin's resolve. He scanned the horizon, searching for the silhouettes of Proctor's cohorts, but the prairie remained eerily quiet, save for the rustle of the wind through the tall grass.

With a steely glare, Odin cocked the hammer back on his rifle, the sound sharp and defiant. "You wanna go to Hell? Let's go there together," he declared, his voice steady despite the adrenaline coursing through his veins. The heat of the midday sun bore down on him, but he felt a coolness within—the calm before the storm. Proctor's eyes narrowed, a predator sizing up its prey, and Odin could see the madness flickering behind them. It was a showdown no one in their right mind would want, but Odin had never been one to back down from a fight.

Jolly sat in the shade of a sprawling oak tree, his Henry rifle resting on his knee as he scanned the horizon. The sun cast dappled shadows on the ground, creating a cool spot perfect for waiting. He was deep in thought, contemplating the movements of the three hunters he knew were lurking nearby. Their presence made the woods tense, and every rustle of leaves sent a shiver down his spine. Just then, he heard hurried footsteps approaching, and he spun around, ready to react.

There stood Challi, his young friend, panting and wide-eyed. Jolly's heart raced for a moment, and he lowered his rifle in relief. "Crazy squirt, I liked to have shot ya! What are you doing here?" he barked, though his voice carried an undertone of concern. Challi looked down at his feet, shuffling nervously as if he were on the verge of tears. Jolly felt a pang of empathy; the boy had a knack for finding trouble, and today was no exception.

"Alright, alright," Jolly sighed, his annoyance fading as he saw the fear in Challi's eyes. "You can stay with me, but you gotta be quiet. Those other three are somewhere close, you bet your bottom dollar." Challi nodded eagerly, a small smile breaking through his earlier distress. Jolly motioned for him to sit beside him, and the two settled into the quietness of the woods, hearts racing with the thrill of the hunt and the lurking danger that surrounded them.

As the minutes ticked by, Jolly kept his eyes peeled for any sign of the three hunters. He could feel Challi's fidgeting beside him, a ball of energy contained in a still body. "You gotta learn to be still, Challi," he whispered, glancing sideways at the boy. "If they see us, it could be trouble." Challi nodded vigorously, his eyes wide as he took a deep breath, trying hard to follow Jolly's advice. Together, they waited, listening to the symphony of nature—the chirping of crickets, the rustling leaves, and the distant call of a bird.

Suddenly, a loud crack echoed through the trees, and Jolly's instincts kicked in. He raised his rifle, scanning the area. Challi's hand gripped Jolly's sleeve tightly, a fearful breath escaping his lips. "Stay low," Jolly whispered, his heart pounding as he prepared for whatever might come next. The woods were alive with mystery and danger, and the bond between the two boys was strengthened in that moment of uncertainty, as they braced themselves against the unknown together.

Suddenly, the stillness shattered as gunfire erupted in a chaotic symphony. The acrid scent of gunpowder filled the air, mingling with the dust that rose around them. Odin fired back with unwavering determination, each shot a testament to his grit. But as the bullets flew, Odin's gaze remained locked on Proctor. The man was a tempest, driven by a thirst for bloodshed and conquest, and Odin knew he had to end this before it spiraled out of control.

As the dust settled and the echoes of gunfire faded, Odin emerged from the fray, breathless but unyielding. Proctor lay on the ground, dying, his eyes filled with a mix of rage and disbelief. Odin approached cautiously, the rifle still trained on him. "You thought you could take me down, didn't you?" he murmured, a hint of triumph in his voice. The other three men shouted over to Proctor to see if he needed help their fight had been about more than survival; it was about standing firm in the face of darkness, and Odin had emerged victorious, if only for this moment.

Odin stood in the fading light of the day, rifle slung across his shoulder, a smirk curling at the corners of his lips. The air was thick with the scent of gunpowder and tension, remnants of a confrontation that had spiraled out of control. He looked over at his two companions, Jolly and Challi, who were crouched behind a weathered boulder, their eyes wide with a mix of fear and adrenaline. Dusty stood at his side, growling softly, sensing the unease that hung in the air like a storm cloud.

"Proctor?" asked one of the three men.

"Naw, he met his maker, you wanna try?" Odin quipped, his voice steady as he cocked his rifle again, eyes narrowing at the three men who had come too close for comfort. They were buffalo hunters, their intentions clear, and the glint of their weapons betrayed their sinister motives. Dusty barked, a low, warning growl that echoed off the cliffs around them. With a swift motion, Odin raised his rifle, his finger poised on the trigger, and fired. The echo of the gunshot rang out, one after another, as the three men fell like puppets cut from their strings.

Chapter 7

For a moment, silence enveloped the scene, broken only by the distant call of a crow circling overhead. Dusty trotted forward, sniffing the ground where the buffalo hunters had fallen, as Odin kept a watchful eye, ready for any sign of life. The adrenaline coursed through him, a mix of relief and triumph. "Looks like we've dealt with our problems," he said, a hint of bravado in his voice, though he felt the weight of what he had just done pressing down on his conscience.

Just then, Jolly and Challi emerged from their hiding spot, wide-eyed and breathless, their faces pale. "What just happened?" Jolly asked, disbelief etched on his features. Challi, still clutching his bow and arrow, took a tentative step forward. He whispered in Sioux, his voice trembling. Odin nodded, trying to project confidence even as he felt the shadows of doubt creep into his mind. He had acted without hesitation, but the gravity of taking lives was not lost on him.

As the sun dipped below the horizon, casting long shadows across the land, Odin knew they had survived another day in a world that demanded toughness and quick decisions. Yet, deep within, he could feel the weight of his actions lingering, a reminder that survival often came at a cost. Dusty returned to his side, nuzzling him gently, a comforting presence amidst the chaos. Together, they stood, watching the last rays of sunlight fade, knowing that tomorrow would bring new challenges, but for now, they had each other, and that was enough.

Odin squinted as the sun cast golden rays over the dusty road that stretched ahead of them. "How many miles till we get to Red River?" he asked, a hint of impatience creeping into his voice. The endless expanse of dirt road felt like a never-ending ribbon, and the excitement of their destination tugged at his thoughts.

"Five miles," Jolly replied. He had always been the optimistic one, always seeing the bright side of every journey. The three friends were on an adventure, with the promise of cool waters and a peaceful afternoon waiting for them at the Red River.

As they galloped along, the scenery began to shift. Golden fields of wheat swayed gently in the wind, and the distant mountains loomed like guardians of their destination. Five miles seemed to vanish like the clouds drifting across the sky. Soon, they would arrive, and the thrill of their impending escapade filled the air, promising a day of carefree joy at Red River.

****

Red River, Dakota Territory

As the sun began to set, painting the sky in hues of orange and purple, Jolly, Odin, Challi and Dusty trudged through the dense forest, their destination finally in sight. They had heard tales of the treacherous river that lay ahead, and now, as they approached its banks, a figure loomed on the opposite side. An old hag, with a crooked nose and wild hair, stood waiting for them. It was Granny Hatchet, known for her uncanny ability to ferry people across the waters. Her spitting tobacco created a sticky trail that dripped down her weathered face, but she seemed unfazed, wiping it off with her grimy sleeve.

"Look, Jolly, it's your woman. Pucker up," Odin chuckled, nudging Jolly with a smirk. "You go to hell," said Jolly rolling his eyes, knowing full well that Granny Hatchet had a reputation that preceded her. The stories of her sharp tongue and even sharper hatchet were enough to send shivers down anyone's spine. Yet, they needed her help to cross the river, and there were no other options. As they approached the water's edge, Granny beckoned them closer with a crooked finger, her eyes gleaming with mischief.

"Got gold, Boys?" she croaked, her voice gravelly like the stones beneath their feet. Jolly fumbled through his pockets, producing a few coins, which seemed to amuse her. "That won't buy you much!" she cackled, exposing a set of yellowed teeth. "But I'll take you across, if you're brave enough to face the currents." Jolly exchanged glances with Odin, both of them weighing their options. Dusty ran across as Challi stepped down and pulled the reins of the horses and mare mule aboard the raft. The river was notorious for its whirlpools, and

Granny's ferry was a rickety old boat that seemed to have seen better days.

With a resigned sigh, Jolly stepped into the boat, followed closely by Odin. Granny spit into the river. "Sweetness, stay close to me. As for the rest of you hunker down," said Granny flirting with Jolly. He shivered slightly, not just from the chill in the air but also from a mixture of fear and awe toward the old woman who seemed to command the river itself. As they pushed off from the shore, the water splashed against the sides, a chilling reminder of the danger that lay ahead. Granny cackled as she rowed, her laughter echoing like a sinister melody across the water.

Granny cackled as she took hold of the oars, her laughter echoing like a sinister melody across the water. "Hold on tight, boys! The river has a mind of its own!" she shouted, her voice barely containing the wild excitement that set Jolly's heart racing. The boat rocked violently, and Jolly clutched the sides, his knuckles turning white. It felt as if the very spirit of the river was awakening, eager to reveal its secrets to those brave enough to traverse its depths.

As they ventured further into the winding waters, strange shapes began to materialize beneath the surface, shadows that danced with the current. Jolly and Odin exchanged nervous glances, their imaginations running wild with thoughts of mythical creatures and ancient tales. Granny, however, seemed unfazed, her eyes sparkling with mischief as she regaled them with stories of the river's legendary past. "Many have come before you," she said, her voice low and mysterious, "but not all have returned." The weight of her words hung heavy in the air, amplifying the thrill and terror of their journey.

Just as the sun dipped below the horizon, painting the sky with hues of orange and purple, a sudden storm brewed on the water. Thunder rumbled overhead, sending ripples of fear through Jolly's heart. But Granny remained steadfast, her laughter ringing out defiantly against the encroaching chaos. "This is where the fun begins!" she declared, steering the boat with an uncanny grace, as if she were dancing with the tempest. Jolly felt a rush of adrenaline; this was not just a journey down a river, but a rite of passage, an adventure that would forge unbreakable bonds between the three of them.

As the storm unleashed its fury, the boat crested waves like a wild stallion, and Jolly realized that he was no longer afraid. With Granny's unwavering guidance and Odin's determined spirit beside him, he found strength in the heart of the storm. The river, once a daunting abyss, transformed into a canvas of awe and exhilaration. Together, they embraced the chaos, knowing that this adventure would be etched into their memories forever, a testament to their courage and the whimsical magic of Granny Hatchet.

As the sun dipped low over the Red River, casting a warm glow on the water's surface, Granny's keen eyes caught sight of movement along the bank. Seven men were shadowing them, their silhouettes cutting sharp lines against the fading light. With a furrowed brow, Granny turned to Odin. "Friends of yours?" she asked, her voice steady despite the impending danger.

Odin squinted at the figures advancing behind them. Digger and Hawk were unmistakable, their rugged faces familiar but far from welcome. With five other men in tow, they were clearly up to no good. "No, we gotta lose them," he replied urgently. The river churned with a sense of foreboding as they pushed forward, the sound of hooves and the rush of water blending into a cacophony of tension. "Can we get further downriver before they catch up?"

Granny's gaze flicked to the floorboard of the ferry, where an old wooden box sat. "See that box, there sitting on the floorboard? It's my rifle, get it for me," she commanded, her tone leaving no room for argument. Odin's heart raced; he had always underestimated the old woman, but her steely determination was evident. Without hesitation, he reached for the box, feeling the weight of the rifle inside as he handed it to her.

As Granny readied the rifle, her fingers deftly tracing the worn wood, the urgency of their situation hung heavy in the air. The river surged on, but Granny was unyielding. She had faced worse than these men before, and she wasn't about to back down now. "Hold on tight, Odin. We'll give them something to remember," she declared, her eyes glinting with fierce resolve. The chase was on, and with every beat of the river, they raced towards an uncertain fate, the Red River their only ally in a standoff that promised to be anything but ordinary.

Granny crouched behind the ferry wheel, her weathered hands steady on the rifle as she peered down the riverbank. "You okay sweetness? Hang on," she called out to Jolly, who was just a few feet away, trying to catch his breath after the chaotic skirmish. "Stop calling me sweetness," said Jolly. As the sun was setting, painting the sky a deep orange, but the shadows cast by the looming trees felt more ominous than beautiful. Jolly's eyes were wide with fear, and his heart raced as he nodded, though he could barely muster a smile.

With a fierce determination, Granny fired a couple of shots into the air, hoping to intimidate Digger and Hawk's men who were gathered along the riverbank. The sound echoed through the canyon, causing the seven men to scatter like startled birds. "That should keep them on their toes," she muttered under her breath, but there was a nagging feeling in her gut. She knew they could retaliate, and the distance between them made it difficult to aim true. The men weren't fools; they would regroup and come back with a vengeance.

Jolly's breathing steadied as he watched Granny, his heart swelling with admiration for the old woman's bravery. But just as he felt a flicker of hope, the sharp crack of gunfire rang out from the other side of the river.

The bullets whizzed past them, kicking up dirt and splintering branches. Granny ducked down, her instincts honed from years of facing danger, but Jolly felt rooted in place, fear locking his feet to the raft. "Get down!" Granny shouted, pulling Jolly down beside her.

The situation was growing desperate. Granny's thoughts raced as she calculated their next move. "We can't stay here forever," she said, her voice low but firm. "We need to find a way to flank them." Jolly nodded, his mind shifting from fear to resolve. "I'll follow your lead," he whispered, the fire of determination igniting within him. Together, they began to whisper a plan, eyes scanning the riverbank for any sign of Digger and Hawk's men, ready to take the fight to them before night fell completely.

As the sun dipped below the horizon, the shadows lengthened, and a new sense of urgency filled the air. Granny and the others exchanged a determined glance, knowing that they would have to rely on each other to survive the night. With hearts pounding, they prepared to leave their cover, ready to confront whatever danger awaited them on the other side of the river.

In the heart of the once-peaceful valley, chaos reigned as the scalp hunters closed in on Granny and her small band of defenders. Odin, Challi, and Jolly stood shoulder to shoulder, their faces etched with a mixture of fear and resolve. The air was thick with the acrid smell of gunpowder, and the sharp crack of gunfire echoed off the mountains. Granny, though advanced in years, was a formidable presence. Her fierce gaze swept over her companions, igniting a fire of determination in their hearts. They were outgunned and outnumbered, but they were not yet defeated.

As the scalp hunters advanced, their jeers mingling with the sound of gunfire, Granny felt a surge of adrenaline. "We must hold the line!" she shouted, her voice steady despite the chaos. Odin nodded, gripping his rifle tightly, while Challi and Jolly scrambled to prepare their defenses. The hunters were targeting Granny's ferry, a vessel that had carried them across the red River many times, and it was now their lifeline. If they lost it, their chances of escape would dwindle to nothing.

With a fierce determination burning in her chest, Granny rallied her forces. "Remember the Alamo!" Her words struck a chord, and the trio found renewed strength. They took positions behind whatever cover they could find, returning fire as best they could. The valley that had once been a place of laughter and song now trembled with the sound of battle. Yet, amidst the turmoil, the spirit of resistance burned brightly in their hearts.

As the battle raged on, Granny devised a plan. "We must create a diversion," she instructed, her mind racing with possibilities. "Challi, you and Jolly draw their fire. With a nod, Challi and Jolly set off, their hearts pounding as they opened fire towards the ridge. Granny felt a sense of pride swell within her; they were fighting not just for survival, but for the very essence of their way of life. The scalp hunters, notorious for their ruthless pursuits, had set their sights on Challi and Jolly.

Without hesitation, she reached for the concealed Gatling gun, her weathered hands moving with surprising agility. As she unleashed a series of gunfire, the sound echoed across the river, startling the birds into flight. Odin, caught off guard by the sudden chaos, was tossed from the deck, his startled yelp swallowed by the din of battle.

Chapter 8

"Granny, you okay?" Jolly called out, his voice barely audible over the noise. He quickly scanned the deck for any signs of danger. Granny shot him a cheeky wink, her spirit as fierce as ever. "Doing well, sweetness," she replied, her laughter mingling with the gunfire. Jolly, emboldened by her confidence, grabbed the Gatling gun and began firing along the banks of the river, each pull of the trigger sending a spray of bullets into the air.

Meanwhile, Hawk crouched low, eyes wide in disbelief. "Damn! Where'd they get a Gatling?" he shouted, his heart racing. The sight of Granny, usually so demure, brandishing a weapon of such ferocity was both terrifying and exhilarating. Digger, ever the pragmatist, grunted in response, "Who cares? Just keep firing and let's hope the old hag doesn't pop up with any more surprises." The urgency in his voice spurred the others into action, their camaraderie forged in the heat of chaos.

As the bullets whirred through the air, the enemy boats on the river began to emerge, their silhouettes stark against the setting sun. Jolly's aim was true, and one by one, they were taken down, splashes of water erupting as the projectiles found their marks. Granny stood her ground, a fierce protector of her crew, her laughter rising above the roar of the Gatling gun. It was a battle unlike any they had ever fought, and in that moment, the old ferry felt like a fortress, with Granny at the helm and her crew ready to defend their home against all odds.

The sun hung low in the sky, casting long shadows over the riverbank where Digger and Hawk stood, watching their men scatter like leaves in the wind. "Look! I didn't sign on to face no Gatling, let's skin out!" one of the scalp hunters had shouted before bolting toward the high country. Digger clenched his fists, anger boiling inside him as he watched the cowardice unfold. "Cowards! You come back here!" Hawk shouted, his voice filled with frustration and disbelief. But the men were already too far gone, their fear driving them deeper into the wild.

"I'll see you in hell, Mister!" Digger called after them, his voice echoing across the river. He had expected more from his crew, men who had chased glory and gold across the rugged terrains, but the sight of the fearsome Gatling was enough to send them running. He turned to Hawk, whose face was set in grim determination. "We can't let them get away with this. We have to stand our ground." Hawk nodded, gripping his rifle tightly. "They'll be a next time. Come on," shouted Digger.

Suddenly, a loud cheer erupted from the ferry, breaking the tension. "Hot damn we did it! That took the fight outta 'em!" Granny cackled joyfully. She turned around and, in a moment of sheer exuberance, planted a big juicy kiss right on Jolly's mouth, tobacco juice and all. Jolly, taken aback, wiped his mouth in disbelief, but the grin on his face suggested he didn't mind the unexpected display of affection.

The sound of their laughter filled the air, momentarily distracting Odin and Jolly from their frustration. Granny had a way of lifting spirits, even in the direst situations. "We may have lost the war," she said, her eyes twinkling with mischief, "but we've made our stand. And that's worth celebrating." Odin couldn't help but smile at her spirit. Maybe they hadn't won the battle today, but they had each other, and that counted for something in this harsh world. As the sun dipped below the horizon, the four of them stood together, ready to face whatever came next, united in their defiance against fear.

Granny turned to Challi and said," here boy take the wheel,". Her wild white hair danced in the wind as she pulled out a weathered jug, its surface etched with runes and symbols only she could decipher. "Care for a snootful?" she asked with a grin, her eyes twinkling like the stars above. Jolly watched in awe, his curiosity piqued by the smell wafting from the jug.

Odin eyeing Granny suspiciously. "What kind of trouble are you brewing this time, Granny?" he called out, his voice gravelly. Dusty darted between Granny's legs, as if he were part of the magical ambiance. "Oh, Brannock, don't be such a sourpuss! This is just a little something to lift the spirits and warm the heart," Granny replied, her laughter bubbling like the concoction inside her jug.

Jolly could hardly contain his excitement. "What does it do, Granny?" he asked, his eyes wide with wonder. "Why, it brings a bit of joy, makes the day brighter, and sometimes even shows you the magic around you!" she answered, pouring a splash of the potion into a tiny cup for him. As he took a sip, the world around him seemed to shimmer, colors becoming more vibrant, and laughter echoing in the distance.

Odin, still skeptical, took a step closer, his curiosity finally getting the better of him. "Maybe just a tiny taste wouldn't hurt," he muttered, his gruff demeanor softening slightly. Granny chuckled as she poured him a small cup, the aroma swirling like a gentle breeze. When Brannock took a sip, a smile crept across his face, and for the first time in ages, he let out a hearty laugh.

As the sun dipped below the horizon, the raft glowed with warmth and laughter. Granny's brew had done more than just lift spirits; it had woven a thread of connection among them, reminding them that sometimes, magic could be found not just in potions, but in the company of friends. The Dakota Territory, once a place of solitude, now thrummed with the joy of shared moments, all thanks to a little snootful of Granny's finest moonshine.

The night was thick with the smell of smoke and the sharp tang of whiskey as Jolly's off-key singing echoed through the dimly lit ferry. His voice, a raucous blend of cheer and clamor, was met with the hearty accompaniment of ol' Granny, who, despite her age, had a spirit that could outshine the moon. The flickering fire cast shadows on the river, dancing to the rhythm of their poorly harmonized tune. Odin couldn't help but chuckle at the scene; it was a bizarre juxtaposition of joy and chaos that had become all too familiar.

Challi watched with wide eyes as Jolly stumbled around, more than a few swigs into the moonshine. He reached for the bottle in his hands, but just as he was about to take a sip, Jolly caught him mid-motion. "You're too young for that!" Jolly exclaimed, laughter bubbling in his voice. The old man, with his beard as wild as the forest and his eyes twinkling with mischief, handed Challi a bottle of whiskey instead. The boy hesitated, glancing at Odin for guidance, but the older man merely shrugged, a smirk creeping across his face.

"Just a taste won't hurt," Odin teased, raising his glass as if to toast the reckless spirit of the night. Jolly winked conspiratorially at Challi, urging him to take the plunge. The ferry filled with laughter as the boy finally took a cautious swig, grimacing at the burn that followed. "See? It's like drinking fire!" Jolly guffawed, clapping Challi on the back, while Granny sang a verse about wild adventures on the Red River.

Despite the merriment, a shadow lingered in Odin's mind. The scalp hunters had been a violent threat. He glanced at Jolly and Granny, their faces flushed with drink and laughter, and felt a pang of worry. Were they truly gone for good, or was this just a brief respite? As the songs continued and the fire crackled, Odin's thoughts drifted, caught between the warmth of camaraderie and the cold grip of uncertainty. The night wore on, and with each off-key note, the world outside seemed to fade, if only for a moment.

****

The morning sun cast a warm glow over the Red River, shimmering on its waters like scattered diamonds. Granny, sturdy and weathered from years of navigating the rough currents of life, expertly maneuvered her ferry to the bank where the ferry line ended. As she hoisted the anchor, she felt a sense of relief wash over her. "This here is where I stop," she declared, her voice firm yet gentle, signaling the end of their journey together for now.

Challi led the horses and the mare mule across the riverbank. Odin with a quick grin and a heart full of adventure, turned to Granny with gratitude shining in his eyes. "Been one helluva ride, Granny, much obliged," he said, a tone of sincerity lacing his words. Granny chuckled, brushing a stray wild white hair from her forehead. "Shoot, it was nothing to it. I enjoyed it myself," she replied, a twinkle in her eye, recalling the excitement of the ride.

As Jolly prepared to depart for land, Granny suddenly grabbed him by the arm. With a swift motion, she whirled him around and planted a kiss on his cheek. "So long sweetness, I'm gonna miss ya," she said, her voice filled with a mix of affection and mischief. Jolly blushed, caught off guard but pleased, a smile creeping onto his lips. "I reckon I will too, especially that witches brew you got with ya," he responded, thinking of Granny's famous concoctions that had kept the chill at bay during their travels.

With the ferry now settled and the horses grazing peacefully, a silence hung in the air, heavy with unspoken words and promises of future adventures. They knew that the journey was far from over; the Red River still held many secrets and stories yet to unfold. Granny waved them off as they stepped onto the shore, her heart full of fond memories, while the river continued its timeless flow, whispering tales of the past and the hope of what was to come.

Odin, Jolly, and Challi reined up their horses on the dusty trail that wound through the sprawling hills. The sun hung low in the sky, casting a golden hue over the landscape, while the gentle breeze whispered through the tall grass. Odin, the eldest of the trio, adjusted his hat against the bright rays, glancing at his companions. Jolly, ever the optimist, flashed a grin, eager for the adventures that lay ahead, while Challi, always practical, checked their supplies, ensuring they were prepared for whatever the wilderness might throw their way.

As they trotted forward, the rhythmic sound of hooves against the earth created a comforting melody. The trio shared stories of their past travels, laughter echoing through the air. Odin spoke of a river he once crossed that sparkled like diamonds under the sun, while Jolly added tales of wild animals they had encountered, his eyes twinkling with excitement. Challi, in contrast, reminded them to be cautious, recounting a time when a careless mistake had nearly cost them dearly. The balance of their personalities made for a harmonious journey, each contributing to the camaraderie that had formed over their years of friendship.

The terrain gradually shifted, the gentle hills giving way to more rugged landscapes. A sense of adventure filled the air, and the thrill of the unknown beckoned them onward. They navigated through narrow passes and over rocky outcrops, the challenges only strengthening their resolve. With each mile, the Dakota Territory revealed its beauty and wildness, a reminder of the untamed spirit that still existed in the world. The trio pressed on, their laughter mingling with the sounds of nature, a testament to their bond as they explored the vast frontier together.

As dusk approached, they found a serene clearing beside a glistening stream. Jolly suggested they set up camp for the night, and Challi nodded, already assessing the best spot for their tent. Odin gathered firewood, his thoughts drifting to the stars that would soon blanket the sky. In this moment of camaraderie and tranquility, they felt a deep connection to the land and each other, their hearts filled with gratitude for the journey they had embarked on. They shared stories around the crackling fire, the Dakota wilderness surrounding them, a silent witness to their adventure.

****

As dawn broke over the horizon, casting a warm glow across the rugged landscape, Jolly, Challi, and Odin along with Dusty prepared for their journey to the Montana Territory. The air was crisp, filled with the scent of pine and earth, as they packed their belongings. Jolly, with a twinkle in his eye, began to sing, his off-key notes echoing through the trees. Challi, not one to be outdone, joined in, his voice harmonizing poorly with Jolly's. Odin rolled his eyes, exasperated by the cacophony. How could a man of Jolly's age have so many songs in his repertoire, each sung with such reckless abandon?

The road ahead was long and winding, stretching out like a ribbon between the mountains. As they rode, the sun climbed higher in the sky, and the trio continued their melodic misadventures. Jolly belted out tales of daring cowboys and lost loves, his voice rising and falling in an unpredictable rhythm. Meanwhile, Challi added his own verses, blending folklore from his people with Jolly's outlandish lyrics. The result was a patchwork of sounds that filled the otherwise quiet wilderness, much to Odin's chagrin.

Despite his irritation, Odin couldn't help but smile at the sight of his companions. Jolly's infectious spirit and

Challi's laughter lightened the heavy atmosphere of their journey. The more they sang, the more the miles seemed to fade away, transforming the solitude of the road into a lively adventure. Each note was a step closer to the Montana Territory, where Challi's people awaited them, and with every song, the bonds of friendship strengthened.

As the day wore on, the landscape shifted, revealing rolling hills and valleys that seemed to stretch endlessly. The sun dipped low in the sky, painting everything in shades of orange and gold. Jolly and Challi, undeterred by their lack of vocal prowess, continued their serenade, their laughter mingling with the sounds of nature. Odin, despite his earlier annoyance, found himself tapping his foot to the rhythm, surrendering to the joy of the moment. With each note, they forged not just a path through the wilderness, but a tapestry of memories that would carry them through the trials ahead.

As dusk settled over the forest, Challi was chosen to fetch firewood for the campfire. The sun dipped below the horizon, casting long shadows among the trees. Dusty trotted beside him, his nose twitching with the scents of the wilderness. Everything seemed calm; the only sounds were the rustling leaves and the distant chirping of crickets. Challi gathered twigs and small branches, feeling a sense of peace in the cool evening air.

Suddenly, Dusty stopped, his body tense and bristles raised. A low growl rumbled from deep within him, a sound that carried both warning and urgency. Challi was gone. Jolly turned to Odin, who had been watching the scene unfold with growing concern. "What's wrong with Dusty?" he asked, his voice barely above a whisper. Odin's gaze flickered to the darkening trees around them. "He senses something," he replied, instinctively moving closer to his friend.

Odin stood at the edge of the forest, his brow furrowed with worry. "Challi!" he hollered, but the echo of his voice faded into the trees, swallowed by the dense underbrush. Silence hung in the air like a heavy curtain, and an uneasy feeling settled in his stomach. Dusty was restless at his side, sniffing the ground and the air, sensing something amiss. Odin glanced down at the eager canine, who seemed more alert than usual, as if he could sense the tension that surrounded them.

"Hey, Jolly," Odin called out, turning to his friend who was busy gathering supplies for their campfire. "You seen Challi?" His voice carried a note of urgency. Jolly looked up from his task, his brow creasing in concern. "Last I saw of him, he was gathering firewood," he replied, his tone shifting from casual to serious. It was unusual for Challi to wander off without a word, especially when they were deep in the woods.

"Best we go look for him," Odin said, determination replacing his worry. He felt a prick of anxiety; the forest was vast and full of secrets. Jolly nodded, his expression mirroring Odin's concern. "Right," he said, and together they set off, Dusty leading the way, his nose to the ground, tail wagging but tense. The trees loomed overhead, their branches intertwining like fingers whispering secrets, as the trio ventured deeper into the thicket.

As they walked, the underbrush crackled beneath their feet, and the air grew cooler. Dusty darted ahead, his instincts guiding him, while Odin and Jolly called out for their missing friend. Each shout felt increasingly futile, as if the forest itself was absorbing their words. The thick canopy above dimmed the sunlight, casting eerie shadows that danced around them, adding to the sense of foreboding.

Minutes turned into what felt like hours, and just when doubt began to creep into Odin's mind, Dusty suddenly stopped, ears perked up, body rigid. Odin and Jolly exchanged worried glances and hurried to catch up. "What is it, boy?" Odin asked, kneeling beside Dusty, who was sniffing intently at a cluster of bushes. Jolly leaned in, eyes wide with curiosity. "Do you think he's nearby?"

Odin and Jolly along with Dusty ventured deeper into the brush, their hearts racing with excitement and a hint of fear. The dense greenery wrapped around them like a living blanket, and the air was filled with the scent of damp earth and wildflowers. As they moved cautiously, Dusty suddenly stopped, his nose twitching in the air. He had spotted something unusual—a large hollow tree trunk nearby, its gnarled roots clutching the ground like ancient fingers. But there was more to this scene than met the eye.

Challi, curious and brave, approached the tree trunk. Dusty raced to get to his side as his growl grew louder and more frantic. It was a sound that sent shivers down Challi's spine. The rustling outside the brush became more pronounced, a warning that something was lurking nearby. Dusty's instincts kicked in; he sensed danger. Suddenly, the bushes parted, and out sprang an old mountain lion, its golden eyes locked onto Challi with a predatory intensity. In a moment of pure instinct, Challi dashed toward the hollow tree trunk, seeking refuge from the looming threat.

The rough bark scraped against Challi's back as he pressed himself inside the trunk, heart pounding like a drum in his chest. He could hear the mountain lion prowling outside, its heavy breathing mingling with the sounds of the forest. Reaching the tree trunk, Dusty spotted the intruder. He raced to get infront of the hollow tree, while standing guard at the entrance, barking fiercely, trying to fend off the majestic but terrifying creature that had cornered his friend. The tension hung in the air like a thick fog, every sound amplified in the quiet wilderness.

Inside the hollow trunk, Challi felt a strange mix of fear and exhilaration. He was safe for the moment, but he could hear the mountain lion pacing back and forth, its presence a constant reminder of the danger lurking just outside. Dusty, ever the protector, would not abandon him. Challi could see the silhouette of the lion through the branches, a magnificent beast that commanded respect. He realized that this encounter was not just about survival; it was a lesson in the wild's unforgiving nature.

As time passed, the mountain lion eventually lost interest, its growls fading into the distance. Dusty relaxed slightly, though his eyes remained alert. Challi let out a breath he didn't know he was holding and emerged from the trunk, rejoining his faithful companion. Together, they took one last look at the wild beauty around them before making their way back home, forever changed by their brush with danger, their bond stronger than ever. The adventure had deepened their understanding of the wilderness, a reminder of both its beauty and its peril.

Before Odin and Jolly could ponder further, a rustle came from the bushes, and Challi emerged, his face smeared with dirt and a branch in his hand and Dusty alongside him. He spoke in Sioux about the terrible ordain. Relief washed over Odin and Jolly. Dusty barked happily, bouncing around Challi. "We were worried sick about you!" Odin scolded good-naturedly, shaking his head. Challi shrugged, still buzzing with excitement.

Challi stood in the clearing, the sun filtering through the leaves above, casting dappled shadows on the forest floor. Jolly had been scolding him for wandering too far from their camp. "You need a good whipping boy....but you're safe that's the main thing, don't wander off again," Jolly said, a mix of relief and frustration in his voice. Challi nodded, his eyes wide with a mix of curiosity and guilt, knowing he had worried Jolly. Just then, a loud crack echoed through the woods, and a towering tree, twisted and ancient, came crashing down behind him.

The ground trembled slightly, and Jolly's heart raced as he spun around, fearing for Challi's safety. But when he turned back, he saw Challi standing there, unharmed, a look of astonishment on his face. He spoke in Sioux as if to say, "I'm okay! I didn't even move," Challi exclaimed, excitement bubbling in his voice, as if the near miss had only ignited his adventurous spirit further. Jolly and Odin let out a sigh of relief, his worry dissipating like mist in the morning sun. He approached Challi, placing a hand on his shoulder. "Next time, just stay close, alright? This place can be unpredictable."

From behind the tree that had just fallen, was a burly French figure emerged, axe in hand, his rough features set in a determined expression. It was Milo Devereux. "Didn't mean to startle you boys," Milo said with a hearty laugh, wiping sweat from his brow. "Just clearing out some of these old trees before they fall and cause a real mess. Lucky I got here in time!" His presence was reassuring, and Challi felt a thrill at having such a brave figure nearby.

Odin stood there, his muscles tense and ready for action. The air was thick with tension as he faced Milo, who was casually leaning against a weathered log. "You're stupid! You could've killed us," Odin shouted, his voice echoing through the forest. The shadows danced around them, creating an atmosphere charged with uncertainty. It was clear that the situation had escalated, and Odin's patience had worn thin.

Milo shrugged, a nonchalant grin plastered across his face. "Oh, come on, Odin. It was just a little miscalculation," he replied, his tone dripping with sarcasm. He had always been the reckless one, taking risks that left Odin frustrated and furious. As the two men stood in stark contrast, the weight of their friendship hung in the air, tested by a moment of near disaster.

Odin took a deep breath, trying to quell the anger bubbling inside him. He could feel the adrenaline coursing through his veins, a reminder of how close they had come to tragedy. "You don't get it, do you? It's not just about you, Milo. Your actions have consequences," he said, his voice steadying as he fought to keep his emotions in check. The thought of what could have happened haunted him, and he couldn't shake the image of disaster from his mind. As they chatted, the forest seemed to come alive, the sounds of birds and rustling leaves creating a symphony around them.

Milo's expression shifted slightly, the carefree facade faltering for a moment. "I know, I know," he admitted, his bravado fading. "But you have to admit, it was exciting!" The tension between them hung in the air, a delicate balance of frustration and camaraderie. In that moment, they both understood that their friendship was built on the edge of chaos, and while Odin often played the role of the cautious protector, Milo thrived in the unpredictable storm of life.

With a reluctant chuckle, Odin finally relaxed his clenched fists. "Exciting doesn't begin to cover it, you lunatic. Just promise me you'll think before you act next time." Milo nodded, a mischievous grin returning to his lips. They both knew that despite the chaos, they wouldn't have it any other way.

Jolly, feeling more at ease now, exchanged stories with Milo about the many adventures they had encountered since they last saw each other. Challi listened intently, his earlier fears forgotten, replaced by dreams of future escapades with his friends. The day's close encounter had turned into a lesson on safety, friendship, and the untamed beauty of nature, reminding them all of the bonds that held them together, even in the face of danger.

Milo was at it again, his mischievous spirit dancing like a flickering candle in the wind. Just moments ago, he had nearly caused a fatal accident that left Odin fuming, and now the tension in the air was as thick as a fog rolling over a sleepy harbor. Jolly, ever the loyal supporter of Milo, stood in between the two, his hands raised in a gesture of peace. "There's no harm done, Milo was just being Milo," he said, his voice light and cheerful, as if trying to sweep away the storm that brewed between his friends.

Odin crossed his arms, glaring at Milo with a mix of annoyance and disbelief. He had grown weary of Milo's antics, which often teetered on the edge of mischief and mayhem. "You call this harmless?" he retorted, pointing to the fallen tree that had landed squarely next to Challi. "This isn't just a joke, Jolly. It's getting old." Jolly, however, remained undeterred, his affection for Milo coloring his view. "You know how he gets," he chuckled, trying to lighten the mood. "Now come on, let's all be friends."

Despite Odin's irritation, he couldn't suppress a small smile at Jolly's unwavering optimism. There was something endearing about how Jolly always stood up for Milo, even when he was clearly in the wrong. Perhaps it was the way Jolly's eyes sparkled with admiration whenever Milo pulled off a stunt, or the way he laughed, a sound that seemed to wrap around the chaos like a warm blanket. "I suppose you're right," Odin finally sighed, relenting. "But Milo needs to learn when to stop."

Milo, sensing the shift, lowered his head, a sheepish grin playing on his lips. "Alright, I promise to think twice next time," he said, his tone sincere. Jolly clapped him on the back, their friendship as resilient as ever. The three of them stood together, laughter bubbling up as the earlier tension faded like a distant memory. Perhaps this was just another day in their unpredictable lives, but Jolly knew that as long as they had each other, the mischief and mayhem would always be balanced by moments of laughter and friendship.

Jolly and his friends sat around the smoldering campfire, the smoke curling into the twilight sky. They watched as Milo gathered his horse. "You shouldn't let Milo get to ya, Odin," Jolly said, a grin plastered across his face, trying to lighten the mood. But Odin's frown deepened as he cleared the remnants of their fire, his brow furrowed with concern. "Can it, Jolly. It was dangerous and stupid. He ought to know better than to chop down trees and let them fall wherever they land without a care. What if Challi had been killed? Then what?" Odin's voice was measured, each word steeped in the weight of responsibility.

Jolly sighed, his playful demeanor faltering under Odin's serious gaze. He knew Odin was right; the woods were unpredictable, and Milo's antics often put them all at risk. Challi had been collecting firewood nearby, blissfully unaware of the potential danger. The thought alone sent a shiver down Jolly's spine. As the last embers flickered out, the group fell into an uneasy silence, each lost in their thoughts about the daring choices they made in the wilderness. They shared a bond of friendship, yet in moments like this, the fragility of life reminded them of their responsibilities to one another.

****

Challi, Jolly, and Odin had been journeying for days, their feet weary from the long trek across the vast, golden fields. The sun hung high in the sky, casting a warm glow on their adventure. As they rode, laughter and stories filled the air, creating a bond that grew stronger. Soon they came to a lake. After several hours of riding, they finally spotted the shimmering water in the distance.

Upon reaching the lake, the trio was amazed at its beauty. They stepped down from their horses and mare mule. The surface sparkled like diamonds in the sunlight, and the gentle breeze created ripples that danced across the water. Challi, curious by nature, leaned closer to the edge and gazed into the lake. His reflection stared back at him, and he felt a strange pull, as if the water was calling his name. Without thinking, he reached out to touch the surface, but the moment his fingers brushed the water, he lost his balance and fell in with a loud splash.

Jolly watched in shock as Challi disappeared beneath the surface. Panic surged through him as he called out, "Challi! Where are you?" His voice echoed in the serene surroundings, but there was no answer. Odin, who had been collecting branches nearby, heard Jolly's cries and rushed to his side. Together, they searched frantically for any sign of their friend. "We have to help him!" Jolly exclaimed, his heart racing with fear.

Thinking quickly, Odin spotted a sturdy tree branch nearby. "Grab that!" he shouted to Jolly. With teamwork, they stretched the branch out towards the water where Challi had fallen. Challi, struggling to keep afloat, managed to grab hold of it, his face breaking through the surface for a brief moment, gasping for air. With all their strength combined, along with Dusty who had gripped his jaws; Jolly and Odin pulled on the branch, slowly bringing their friend back to safety.

Finally, Challi emerged from the water, dripping wet but alive. He coughed and sputtered, then laughed nervously as he looked at his friends. Speaking in Sioux he chuckled. Jolly and Odin sighed in relief, their hearts finally calming. They had faced a scare, but their friendship had only grown stronger through the ordeal. As they sat by the lakeside, they shared stories of bravery and laughter, grateful for the adventure and for each other.

****

Odin stood on the sandy shore, the sun casting long shadows across the ground as he unfurled an old, weathered map. Jolly leaned over his shoulder, squinting at the faded lines that crisscrossed the paper. "Looks like we need to head north," Jolly suggested, tapping a finger on a drawn mountain range. Meanwhile, Challi was engrossed in a lively game with Dusty, his laughter ringing out as he tossed a small, limb back and forth, oblivious to the serious discussions of the adults.

After a moment, Odin turned to the group, a determined look on his face. "Alright, everyone, we should get moving," he declared, folding the map with care. Challi, hearing the call to adventure, paused her game and rushed over, her eyes sparkling with excitement. Dusty followed closely, still wagging his tail as if he were part of the mission.

Odin reached for the mare mule, who stood patiently nearby, her ears perked up in anticipation. "Challi, it's time for you to ride," he said with a smile, leading the mule closer. Challi beamed, her hands gripping the saddle as she climbed up, feeling the comforting sway of the mare beneath her. Jolly gave her a supportive nod, and Dusty barked happily, ready to trot alongside them.

With everyone settled and the map tucked safely away, Odin took the lead, guiding the group along the path that wound through the trees. Jolly fell into step beside him, discussing the best routes to take, while Challi and Dusty shared stories of their adventures.

Windy Springs, Dakota Territory

Odin and his friends, Jolly, Dusty, and Challi, journeyed through the rugged terrain of the Dakota Territory, their excitement palpable as they approached Windy Springs, a small community nestled between towering mountains. The air was crisp, and the scent of pine trees filled their lungs. As they rode, their voices echoing against the rocky cliffs. They had heard tales of Windy Springs' charm—a place where time seemed to stand still, and the beauty of nature was unmatched.

Upon arriving, the friends marveled at the quaint houses that dotted the landscape, each with its own unique character. The mountains loomed majestically in the background, providing a stunning backdrop to their adventure. They decided to explore the community, eager to meet the locals and discover what made Windy Springs special. The sun began to set behind the peaks, casting a warm glow that enveloped them in a sense of wonder and possibility, marking the beginning of a memorable chapter in their journey together.

No sooner had they arrived of the bustling town than they came in contact with Milo Devereux. Odin pulled back on the reins, halting Thor, his loyal steed. The air was thick with the scent of spices and the sounds of merchants hawking their wares. "Well, well, well, if it isn't Milo," Odin said, his voice laced with a mixture of surprise and annoyance.

Milo stood tall and confident. He spoke in French, his tone casual yet carrying an undercurrent of tension. "It's good to see ya again, Odin," he replied, though the flicker of a smirk on his lips belied any warmth in his greeting. Jolly, riding alongside Odin, chuckled. "What are you doing here?" he asked, his eyes narrowing as he sized up the unexpected encounter.

Milo shrugged, the smirk never leaving his face. "Business, my friends. You know how it goes." He gestured towards a nearby stall overflowing with exotic goods, the vibrant colors almost dazzling in the late afternoon sun. Odin remained wary, knowing that Milo's business often danced along the edges of legality. The bond they once shared had frayed over the years, and now it felt like they were two ships passing in the night, each with their own agenda.

As the conversation continued, the atmosphere grew charged with unspoken words and past grievances. Jolly, ever the mediator, attempted to lighten the mood. "Come on, Milo. We're just passing through. Why not share a drink?" he suggested, his jovial nature at odds with the tension. But Milo's gaze shifted to Odin, assessing whether the old friendship could rekindle or if it was best left in the past, like the dust trailing behind them on the road.

With a reluctant sigh, Odin finally relented. "Alright, let's grab that drink," he said, his voice steadying. Perhaps this unexpected meeting could lead to something more than just old rivalries. As they rode towards the stall, the sun dipped lower in the sky, casting long shadows that seemed to whisper secrets of their shared history, hinting at a night that could either mend or further unravel their ties.

The bustling village square, the scent of roasted meats and sweet pastries filled the air as villagers gathered for the annual harvest festival. Laughter and music rang out, but midst the cheer, a challenge was brewing.

"Forget the drink! Let's find out how good we are, like in the old days!" Milo shouted, his voice booming over the crowd. The villagers turned their attention to the two men, sensing the tension that was about to unfold. Odin, who had always preferred to avoid confrontation, felt a stirring deep within him. The laughter of the villagers faded as he considered Milo's challenge. Could he really stand against the bravado of his friend? The thought of proving himself began to ignite a fire in Milo's heart.

With a reluctant nod, Milo stepped forward, the weight of the challenge settling over him. The villagers formed a circle, eager to witness the contest. Odin set the rules, his voice ringing with confidence. "We shall throw our axes at the target set in the distance. Whoever hits the center most times will be declared the champion!" he declared.

The crowd murmured with excitement, eager to witness the clash of skill between the two men. Milo, still hesitant, accepted the challenge, knowing he had a reputation to uphold. The stakes were high, but so was the tension in the air.

Milo was already boasting about his past victories, while Odin took a deep breath, steadied his nerves, and focused on the task ahead. As the first ax flew from Odin's hand, the crowd erupted in cheers, the blade striking the target with a satisfying thud. When it was Milo's turn, he approached the throwing line with a calm demeanor, drawing on the countless hours spent practicing in solitude. With a steady hand and a focused mind, he released the ax, watching as it soared through the air. It struck the target with precision, landing inches from the bullseye. Gasps echoed from the crowd, and for a moment, silence reigned as everyone processed what they had just witnessed. The balance of the contest had shifted, and for the first time, Odin's confidence wavered.

As the contest continued, it became clear that this was more than just a test of skill; it was a moment of camaraderie and growth for both men. With every throw, Milo gained confidence, and Odin learned the value of humility.

By the end of the contest, it was clear that Milo had matched, if not surpassed, Odin's skill. The crowd erupted in applause, celebrating Milo's unexpected victory. Odin, taken aback, felt the weight of his arrogance crashing down. Instead of accepting defeat gracefully, he stormed away, vowing to train harder and return to reclaim his glory. The villagers cheered not just for the spectacle of the contest, but for the bond that had grown stronger in the face of challenge, celebrating the spirit of friendship forged in the fire of competition.

Jolly and Milo strolled down the dusty street, laughter echoing between them as they reminisced about old times. The sun hung low in the sky, casting a warm golden hue over the town. "Now how about that drink?"

Jolly asked, his eyes sparkling with anticipation. Milo nodded, a grin stretching across his face. They had spent years apart, each carving out their own path, but the bond of friendship had remained unbroken. The saloon was just a few paces away, its rustic wooden sign swaying gently in the evening breeze.

"Come along, Challi," called Odin, who had just caught up with the duo, a playful glint in his eye. Dusty trotted beside him, his tail wagging enthusiastically. The camaraderie among the four friends was palpable, each step towards the saloon filled with the promise of good times and shared stories.

As they entered the saloon, the familiar scent of aged wood and spilled beer wrapped around them like an old blanket. The atmosphere was lively, filled with the sound of clinking glasses and vibrant conversations. They found a corner table, and soon their drinks were ordered—ice-cold beers for the men and a bowl of water for Dusty. The warmth of the place and the joy of reunion made them forget the long years that had passed since they last gathered around a table.

"Remember that time we got lost on our way to church?" Milo began, his laughter contagious. The others leaned in, eager to hear the tale. Jolly and Odin chimed in, each adding their own embellishments to the story, transforming a simple adventure into a legendary escapade. Dusty, oblivious to the hilarity, lay contentedly at their feet, enjoying the camaraderie and the occasional scratch behind her ears.

As the night wore on, the drinks flowed and the stories became more outrageous, each man trying to outdo the other. Odin, with a twinkle in his eye, recounted a wild encounter with a bear that had everyone in stitches. Jolly, never one to back down, followed with a tale of an ill-fated fishing trip that ended with a broken boat and a long swim back to shore. The laughter echoed through the saloon, drawing the attention of other patrons who couldn't help but smile at the group's infectious energy.

Finally, as the evening came to a close and the stars twinkled brightly outside, the friends leaned back in their chairs, satisfied and full of warmth. "To friendship," Jolly raised his glass, and the others followed suit. In that moment, it wasn't just about the drinks or the tales; it was about the bond they shared, the memories they had created, and the promise of many more adventures to come. The saloon may have been just a stop along their journey, but it was a testament to the enduring spirit of friendship that would carry them forward, no matter where life took them next.

Challi sat listening to Milo's French dialect, the shadows dancing around him like ghosts of the past. His mind wandered, piecing together fragments of memories that had long been buried. The face of Milo flashed before him, a fleeting image that sent a chill down his spine. Why did it bother him so much? Then it struck him like a thunderclap—Milo was one of the scalp hunters, the very ones who had murdered his mother on that fateful day. The realization hit him hard, igniting a mix of anger and sorrow that had been simmering beneath the surface for years.

Odin, his loyal friend, noticed the change in Challi's demeanor and tugged at his fringe shirttail, seeking his attention. The boy turned to look down at Challi, confusion etched on his face as Challi began to rattle on in Sioux, words tumbling from his lips like a river overflowing its banks. Odin tried to make sense of the hurried speech, but the language was foreign to him, a barrier that left him feeling helpless. Challi's heart raced as he spoke, wrestling with the burden of his past, determined to confront the shadows that haunted him.

Jolly sat in the dimly lit saloon, the air thick with tension. He had just finished talking to Milo, the sharp knife resting near him in Odin's sheath. The flickering light above cast shadows that danced across the walls, but it was the sudden movement that caught his eye. Challi appeared wild and frantic. His eyes were wide, almost glowing with a feverish intensity, and Jolly felt a shiver run down his spine. He turned just in time to see Challi snatch Odin's cutting knife from Odin's hip.

"Challi, wait!" Jolly yelled, his voice cutting through the heavy silence. But it was too late; Challi was already sprinting towards Milo, who had been sitting quietly at the table, immersed in his own thoughts. Jolly's heart raced as he realized the danger. Challi, usually jovial and carefree, seemed transformed into a figure of wrath, an embodiment of chaos. The knife glinted ominously in the light, and Jolly's instincts kicked in.

Milo looked up, confusion etched across his face. "Challi? What are you doing?" he asked, his tone a mix of concern and disbelief. But Challi's expression was unreadable, a storm brewing behind his eyes. Jolly felt an overwhelming urge to protect his friend, to pull him back from the edge of whatever dark precipice he was teetering on. He rushed forward, arms outstretched, hoping to intervene before things escalated further.

"Please, Challi, put the knife down!" Jolly pleaded, his voice strained. He could feel the weight of the moment pressing down on him, as if the very air around them was charged with electricity. The saloon, once a place of comfort and warmth, now felt like a battleground. Jolly took another step closer, trying to gauge Challi's state of mind. He needed to reach him, to remind him of the friendship they had built over years, rather than let this moment destroy everything.

Challi hesitated for a fraction of a second, his grip on the knife faltering. Jolly seized the opportunity. "This isn't you!" Jolly's words hung in the air, laden with the weight of their shared history. He could see the flicker of recognition in Challi's eyes, a momentary crack in the armor of rage that had encased him. Yet, it was fleeting, as shadows quickly reclaimed their hold.

Just when it seemed that Jolly might pull Challi back from the brink, a loud crash interrupted the tension. Odin turned around, surprised. "Challi, give me the knife," he exclaimed, his gaze darting between the three friends. The sight of the knife and the turmoil in the room jolted him into action. Odin quickly stepped between Challi and Milo, positioning himself as a shield. "Challi, put the knife down! We can talk about this!" he urged, his voice steady despite the chaos surrounding them. The room held its breath, waiting for Challi's next move, as Jolly hoped desperately for a resolution that would bring them all back together.

Odin stood in the dim light of the saloon, the air thick with tension as he confronted Challi. The knife, once a symbol of vengeance, now lay uselessly embedded in the floor, its purpose lost in the weight of their shared history. Challi's silence was deafening, his dark eyes reflecting a storm of emotions as he grappled with the memories of his past. Odin's heart raced; he knew the gravity of the situation. He repeated his question in Sioux, hoping to break through the wall of grief that Challi had erected around himself. Each attempt was met with an unyielding stare, a refusal to engage that spoke volumes more than words ever could.

Finally, it was the third utterance of the question that pierced the barrier. Challi's voice was a low growl, filled with pain as he recounted the horrors of the scalp hunters who had ravaged his village, the morning his mother was taken from him forever. The weight of his words hung heavy in the air, a mixture of sorrow and wrath that electrified the space between them. Odin understood now; this was not merely about vengeance, but a desperate cry for Sioux justice in a world that had shown none. The knife remained in the floor, a silent witness to the inevitable clash of their destinies, as both men stood at the precipice of a reckoning that would forever change the course of their lives.

"What is with that crazy Injun?" asked Milo in his French dialect staring at Challi.

"So, you were among them, huh." said Odin.

"You going to listen to this Injun rather than your old friend?" asked Milo.

"He lost his family, Milo!" said Odin.

In a quiet corner of the saloon. Jolly stood with his arms crossed, frustration etched on his face. "Now hold on, Odin, we don't know for a fact that it was Milo who killed Squirt's mama, we need to take it easy, and talk this out," said Jolly, trying to diffuse the escalating conflict. Jolly was known for his calm nature and often sought peaceful resolutions, but today, the air was thick with accusation.

"Taking his side again, huh, Jolly? Well, I don't believe him. If Challi said he was among them, then he was," Odin retorted, his voice rising. Dusty, a keen observer with sharp eyes. Challi, had lost his parents to what was believed to be an attack, and the community was on edge, as Odin searched for answers. Challi sat quietly, his tiny heart heavy with grief, hoping that the adults would find Sioux justice for his family.

"Let's not jump to conclusions," Jolly interjected, his voice steady and reassuring. "I saw Milo that morning, but I also saw others. We can't point fingers without knowing the whole truth." He glanced at Challi, whose eyes were filled with tears. Challi had always been protective of the younger ones in the village, and his heart ached for Challi.

Milo, who had been listening quietly, finally spoke up. "I didn't do it! I would never hurt anyone," he pleaded, his eyes wide with desperation. "I was out there cutting down trees and gathering up food. We all know how scarce it gets during the winter." His voice quivered as he looked at the group, hoping they would see the sincerity in his words. The shadows of doubt loomed heavy over him, but he was determined to clear his name.

Odin shook his head, still unconvinced. "We all have to be cautious. If we let Milo go without questioning him, what if he really is guilty? We owe it to Challi to find out the truth!" The tension in the air was palpable as each character wrestled with their emotions. Jolly sighed, feeling the weight of the situation.

****

The sun hung low in the sky, casting long shadows across the dusty streets of the small town. Odin looked sharply at Jolly as they emerged from the saloon. The tension was palpable in the air, thick with unspoken words and the weight of their shared history. "Jolly, you cross me, you'll be just as guilty as he is," Odin warned, his voice low but steady. The words hung between them, a challenge that neither could ignore.

Jolly, a man with a quick wit and a penchant for mischief, smirked but felt the gravity of the situation. He adjusted his hat against the setting sun and nodded, knowing that their quest was not just about loyalty but survival.

Odin stood at the edge of the small town, the sun casting long shadows across the dusty streets. He had always thought of Jolly as a brother in arms, someone who would never turn his back in the face of adversity. But today was different. Today, Jolly had decided to stay behind, a choice that felt like a dagger to Odin's heart. "You coming?" he asked, his voice a mix of surprise and disappointment. He had expected Jolly to ride alongside him, to face whatever lay beyond the horizon together.

"Not this time, old pard, I'm staying here. Got me some thinking to do," Jolly replied, his gaze fixed on the ground as if searching for answers buried in the dirt. Odin could see the turmoil in his friend's eyes, a storm brewing beneath the surface. It was clear that something weighed heavily on Jolly's mind, but Odin couldn't fathom why he would choose contemplation over action, especially with Milo lurking around, always ready to stir trouble.

Odin's frustration bubbled to the surface. He remembered all the battles they had fought side by side, the nights they had shared around a campfire, laughing and plotting their next adventure. How could Jolly abandon that bond now? "Milo's not the kind of guy you want to be alone with, Jolly," he warned, his voice firm. "He'll twist your mind until you don't even recognize yourself." But Jolly merely shrugged, as if the weight of Odin's words was too much for him to carry.

With a heavy heart, Odin turned away, mounting Thor, his faithful steed. He could feel the tension in the air, thick and suffocating. As he rode off, he cast one last glance back at Jolly, who stood motionless, the fading light illuminating his troubled expression. The horizon beckoned him, a place of new beginnings and challenges yet to come. He had to forge ahead, but the thought of leaving Jolly behind gnawed at him.

Chapter 9

Challi ran toward Jolly, his heart heavy with sadness. Jolly had decided not to join them on their journey any longer, and the weight of that decision hung in the air like an unspoken farewell. As he reached his friend, Challi wrapped his arms around him in a tight hug, wishing he could somehow change the course of events. Jolly's eyes were filled with a mix of determination and sorrow, a reflection of the bond they had shared and the adventures that were now left behind.

After a lingering moment, Challi stepped back, his expression shifting to one of resolve. He turned to his mare mule, a sturdy companion that had seen them through countless escapades. With a deep breath, he mounted the mule, feeling the familiar rhythm of her movements beneath him. Though Jolly would not be riding alongside him, Challi was determined to carry their memories forward, hoping that one day, they would share more adventures together. With a nod of farewell, he set off on the path ahead, ready to embrace whatever lay in store, even as he held onto the friendship that had shaped his journey thus far.

Jolly stood at the edge of the rail porch walkway, his heart heavy as he watched Challi and Dusty wagging his tail one last time. "So long, Squirt," he said, trying hard to keep his voice steady, not wanting Challi to see the tears welling in his eyes. Dusty had always been by his side, chasing after sticks, rolling in the grass, and bringing joy to every moment. But now, with his friends moving on toward the Montana Territory, it was time to say goodbye. Jolly bent down to give Challi one last pat, his hand trembling as he fought the urge to cry.

Jolly forced a smile, not wanting to ruin his farewell. He knew he would miss Challi just as much, but the weight of the moment pressed heavily on him. As they prepared to leave, Jolly took one last glance at Dusty, who barked happily, blissfully unaware of the change ahead. With a deep breath, Jolly turned away, hoping that someday, he would find a way to keep the memories of his loyal friends alive, even as new adventures awaited them in the unknown.

As he rode further from the town, Odin's mind raced. He tried to shake off the feeling of betrayal, focusing instead on the path ahead. The landscape shifted from rolling hills to dense woods, the sounds of nature enveloping him. But the nagging worry about Jolly lingered like a shadow, whispering doubts into his ear. What if Milo did manage to corrupt his friend? What if Jolly never found his way back to who he once was?

"Just us, Boy. Might as well get used to it," said Odin, his voice steady as he patted his horse's neck. Challi, perched in the saddle, turned around to glance back at the horizon where the sun dipped low, casting a warm glow over the landscape. He held onto a thread of hope that Jolly would change his mind, that his old friend would come racing after them, laughter trailing in the wind. But as the distance grew, so did the realization that Jolly had made his choice, one he had to respect, even if it gnawed at him from the inside.

The path ahead stretched out like an unending ribbon, winding through trees and over hills. Challi took a deep breath, the scent of pine filling his lungs, but it did little to soothe the ache of loss. He and Odin rode on, the silence between them heavy with unspoken words. They were set to face whatever lay ahead, but the absence of Jolly felt like a ghost haunting their journey. With every step, Challi felt the weight of camaraderie shift, the bond they shared now a fragile thread, stretched thin by the choices they had made.

Days turned into weeks, and Odin fought through various challenges, but he could never escape the feeling that something was off. He often found himself glancing back toward the town, wondering if Jolly was still there, pondering over the very decision that had torn them apart. It was only when he heard whispers of Milo's growing influence that he realized he could no longer sit back. He had to return, confront his fears, and fight for his friend before it was too late. The bond they had shared was worth every risk, and he resolved that he would bring Jolly back, no matter what it took.

As they rode, the sun dipped lower, bathing the land in hues of orange and gold. Odin led the way, his expression fierce and focused. He could feel the weight of responsibility on his shoulders. With Challi riding alongside him, Dusty trotting along. They were heading for mountain country and then over into the Montana Territory. Dusty kept scanning the landscape, ever vigilant, while Challi's mind worked tirelessly, plotting their approach to the mountains.

The sun began to dip below the jagged peaks of the Turtle Mountains, casting long shadows across the rocky terrain. Odin, Challi and Dusty had been riding through the dense underbrush for hours, their bodies weary but their spirits buoyed by the thrill of adventure. They had long heard tales of the riches hidden within the mountains, whispered among the villagers like a sacred incantation. It was said that the mountains were a labyrinth of caves and corridors, guarded by ancient spirits and filled with treasures that sparkled like the stars above. The trio had made a pact—this journey would be theirs to conquer.

As they rode into the twilight, the air grew cooler, carrying with it the earthy scent of moss and fallen leaves. Odin led the way, his eyes darting around, scanning for any signs of danger. "Stay close," he instructed, his voice a soft whisper as if the mountains themselves were listening. Challi attempted to lighten the mood by speaking in Sioux he chuckled, but Odin who was more practical, shot him a serious glance. "This isn't a game, Challi."

The landscape morphed as they ascended a steep incline, the rocky path littered with slick stones and gnarled roots. Each step felt like a small victory, but the sense of unease lingered like a shadow. The stories had also spoken of strange noises echoing through the mountains, of whispers that could lead a traveler astray. Challi paused, his heart racing, as a low rumble reverberated through the ground beneath them. His voice barely above a whisper. Odin rolled his eyes. "It's just the wind," he replied, but even he felt a shiver run down his spine.

Just as they reached the final crest before the mountains loomed above them, the world around them transformed. The sky, previously a warm canvas of oranges and purples, darkened into a deep indigo. Stars began to twinkle, but not just any stars; these seemed to pulse with an otherworldly light. "Look!" Odin exclaimed, pointing to a constellation that flickered more brightly than the rest. It felt as if the universe itself was watching. Intrigued, they moved closer to the edge, where a breathtaking view opened up before them. Below, a shimmering lake reflected the celestial display, its surface smooth as glass.

****

Jolly and Milo were in high spirits that night, their laughter echoing through the dimly lit saloon. The air was thick with the scent of spilled beer and the sounds of clinking glasses. Jolly, with his wild grin and a twinkle in his eye, tossed back another shot, the amber liquid disappearing in a single gulp. Milo, lean and quick-witted, leaned over the table, intent on his cards, his fingers dancing like a magician's as he shuffled the deck. The stakes were high, but the thrill of the gamble was worth every penny they put down.

As the night wore on, the saloon swelled with patrons, each one drawn in by the raucous atmosphere. A group of rowdy men burst into laughter, sharing tales of their escapades, while nearby, a few women, dressed in vibrant skirts and adorned with shimmering jewelry, sat close, their eyes glinting with mischief. Jolly and Milo exchanged glances, their minds racing with possibilities. They were in the heart of the town, where anything could happen, and they were ready to seize the night.

With another round of drinks in hand, the two friends ventured into a game of chance. The dice rolled across the table, their fate hanging in the balance. Jolly's laughter boomed as he won yet again, his pockets growing heavier with each round. But Milo, ever the strategist, had a plan brewing. He was not just there to drink and laugh; he was there to outsmart the room. As he played his cards close to his chest, he noticed the glances exchanged among the women at the bar, their interest piqued by the duo's antics.

As the evening progressed, the saloon's energy shifted; whispers of a high-stakes poker game in a back room reached their ears. Intrigued, Jolly and Milo decided to investigate, hoping to turn their revelry into something more lucrative. The allure of easy money was too enticing to resist. They slipped through a narrow door, finding themselves in a smoky chamber where the stakes were much higher, and the players far more serious. The tension was palpable as they took their seats, ready to gamble not just their coins but their very pride in the uncharted waters of this underground game.

Milo leaned back in his chair, the dim light of the oil lamp casting shadows across the poker table. His fingers idly shuffled the cards as he glanced at Jolly, who was trying to maintain a serious expression amidst the tension of the game. The other players were focused, their brows furrowed in concentration, but Milo couldn't help himself. "To think that an Indian brat would blame me for the killing of his mother, that's ridiculous," he said, the French lilt to his voice betraying a nonchalance that clashed with the gravity of his words. "All they wanted were the scalps; how did I know there was a kid around, Snakefist…"

The table fell silent, eyes darting between Milo and the remaining players, each weighing the implications of his casual admission. Jolly sighed, casting a worried glance at the door as if expecting a vengeful spirit to burst in at any moment. The atmosphere thickened with unspoken tension as Milo, oblivious to the unease he had stirred, continued to play his hand, confident in his abilities. Outside, the wind howled through the cracks in the wooden walls, echoing the turmoil within as the game continued, oblivious to the darker realities that had just been laid bare.

Milo shifted uncomfortably, the weight of his friends' gazes pressing down on him like an anchor. "I didn't mean it like that," he stammered, his face turning a shade of crimson that would put a tomato to shame. Jolly crossed his arms, an eyebrow raised, clearly unconvinced. "Thought you said you hadn't been up there," he repeated, his tone a mix of disbelief and teasing. The "up there" in question was the Sioux village that loomed in the mountains.

Benny, who had been silently munching on peanuts, finally chimed in, "Everyone has to sneak up there at some point." He shrugged, as if this made everything better. Milo remembered the stories they used to share about the village—how it had secret treasures, and how it was the ultimate adventure waiting to be claimed. But now, standing there under the afternoon sun, he felt the weight of his own words sinking deeper into the ground.

Jolly leaned back in his chair, a glint of mischief in his eyes as he played with a deck of cards. "How about it, Milo, you been there or not?" he asked, his tone casual, but his expression hinted at a deeper frustration. Milo, slouched at the table, barely glanced up. "What does it matter? Odin and that brat are gone, and you're here…like old times," he muttered, trying to deflect the conversation. But Jolly's smirk only grew wider, hunger for drama evident in his demeanor.

"What does it matter?" Jolly shot back, his voice rising. "My best pard in the world has taken on the responsibility to take a Sioux boy back to his kin all because you and your friends wanted Indian gold." Benny, perched on the edge of his seat, erupted into laughter, the sound echoing off the wooden walls. "Shut up!" Jolly snapped, his patience thinning. But Milo, determined to make his point, leaned forward. "Jolly, you're not looking at the big picture," he started, but before he could finish, Jolly's fist connected with his jaw, the sharp crack of bone resonating through the room.

As Milo staggered back, Benny's laughter faded, replaced by a tense silence. Jolly, fueled by the thrill of the fight, stood up, ready to escalate the confrontation. "I thought I told you to shut up," he sneered at Benny, who now shifted uncomfortably in his chair. The mood in the room shifted from playful banter to a brewing storm, the anticipation hanging heavy in the air. Milo rubbed his jaw, a fire igniting in his chest. He wasn't going to let Jolly's antics push him around any longer.

With a newfound resolve, Milo straightened up, meeting Jolly's gaze with steely determination. "They're animals. So what if I led them up there into Snakefists's camp, you think I care about Indian gold? I'm done with your games, Jolly," he declared, his voice steady. "Odin may be gone, but I'm not backing down." The saloon, once filled with laughter and camaraderie, now stood witness to a brewing conflict, the friendships hanging by a thread. Benny, caught between the two, felt the weight of the moment, knowing that whatever happened next would change everything.

Benny, Milo, and Jolly stood in the dimly lit saloon, the air thick with tension. Benny felt a rush of excitement as he glanced at Jolly, who seemed lost in thought, staring at the pistol Milo held. Benny knew he couldn't outdraw Jolly himself; there was a certain unease about the way Milo's fingers twitched, suggesting that perhaps he was not as steady as he appeared. It was a risky game they played, one that didn't just involve skill, but also the unpredictable nature of fear.

Milo stood firm, his grip on the gun trembling slightly, but his resolve was clear. "You ready, Jolly?" he asked, his voice steady despite the chaos swirling around them. Jolly finally looked up, his eyes narrowing as he focused on Milo, a mix of determination and apprehension crossing his features. The moment felt suspended in time; each tick of the clock echoed in their hearts as they prepared for the draw.

The challenge was simple yet intense: a test of nerves and precision. Benny's heart raced as he watched the two prepare. He could almost hear the thoughts racing through Jolly's mind, battling between confidence and doubt. The weight of the moment pressed down on them all, and as Benny inhaled deeply, he felt the energy shift in the room. The stakes were high, and for Benny, the thrill of the draw was more than just a game; it was a chance to prove himself through the actions of his friend.

With a shout, they began, the sharp crack of the gun echoing in the saloon. Jolly's shot rang out first, a split second before Milo's hand moved. The bullet found its mark, but it was clear that Milo's hesitation had cost him dearly. As the smoke cleared, Benny couldn't help but feel a mix of relief and disappointment. Milo had faltered, but in that moment, they all learned something vital about courage and the weight of choices. Benny smiled, knowing that sometimes, it was not about who was the fastest, but who could face their fears head-on.

Jolly stood in the dusty saloon, his Colt Navy gleaming in the fading light. He had a reputation as a quick draw, and that made him both respected and feared. The patrons inside the saloon were buzzing with the kind of tension that always came before a storm. Jolly knew Benny was a loose cannon, and as he turned towards the door, he could sense trouble brewing. "Don't even think of touching that gun, Benny, 'cause it'll be the last thing you'll ever do," Jolly warned, his voice steady as he twirled his pistol into his belt.

Benny, a wiry man with a reputation for being reckless, felt the heat of Jolly's glare. But instead of backing down, he was fueled by a reckless bravery. As Jolly turned his back, Benny's fingers twitched towards his pistol, a desperate attempt to assert his dominance.

The moment was electric; the saloon's patrons fell silent, eyes darting between the two men. In a heartbeat, Benny drew his pistol, and the crack of the shot rang out like thunder in the still air.

The bullet struck Jolly in the shoulder, pain searing through him like a wildfire. But even as he felt the life force ebbing, his instincts kicked in. With a swift motion that spoke of years of training, he spun around, his own gun already drawn. The patrons gasped, their hearts racing as they watched the showdown unfold. Jolly fired off two rounds, the bullets finding their mark as Benny staggered backward.

Benny's eyes widened in shock, realizing too late the gravity of his actions. He pitched backward towards the bar, the life draining from him as he collapsed. The saloon erupted into chaos, patrons scrambling for cover, shouting in disbelief. The bartender ducked behind the counter, his hands shaking as he fumbled for his own weapon. The once lively atmosphere turned into a scene of panic, the air thick with the acrid smell of gunpowder.

Jolly stood there, blood seeping through his shirt, his breath coming in ragged gasps. He had survived, but at what cost? He looked down at Benny, who lay lifeless on the floor, the defiance in his eyes extinguished. A heavy silence fell over the saloon as the reality of the situation sank in. Jolly felt a mix of triumph and sorrow; he had won, but he had also lost a piece of himself in the process.

Jolly took a step back, leaning against the wall for support. The bartender peeked over the counter, his expression a mix of fear and admiration. "What now, Jolly?" he asked, his voice barely above a whisper. Jolly looked around at the frightened faces of the patrons, realizing this was a turning point for him. He had to make a choice—would he continue down this path of violence, or could he find a way to redeem himself? The weight of his decision hung heavily in the air, a reminder that every action carried consequences.

Jolly stepped out of the saloon, the heavy wooden doors swinging shut behind him with a creak that echoed in the stillness of the dusty street. He squinted against the bright sun, the heat rising from the ground like a mirage. "Find Odin and Challi," he said, his voice low and urgent as he turned to Shawnee, who was waiting by the hitching post. The urgency in his tone mirrored the rising tension in the small town where secrets seemed to linger just beneath the surface.

Chapter 10

Shawnee nodded in concern. The thought of them gone was unsettling, and Jolly felt a pang of worry for their safety. "We have to hurry," he replied, glancing around the empty street talking to his steed. Jolly swung himself onto his horse, his movements purposeful as he grabbed hold of the saddle horn. The horse snorted, sensing the urgency in its rider. With a quick thrust, he settled into the saddle, his feet dangling just above the stirrups for a moment before he adjusted himself. Jolly set off, the sound of hooves echoing against the wooden buildings lining the street.

As he rode, the landscape around them changed from the bustling town to the open plains, where tall grass swayed in the wind. Jolly led the way, his mind racing with thoughts of Odin and Challi. He replayed their last meeting in his head, trying to remember the details that might give them a clue about where to search. Had they mentioned a location? A plan? The more he thought, the more he realized how little he truly knew about their intentions.

After what felt like hours of riding, he arrived at the edge of a dense forest. The trees loomed high above, their leaves rustling softly in the breeze. Jolly hesitated, looking at Shawnee. With a shared nod, he urged his horse forward into the shadows of the forest. The air grew cooler, the sounds of nature enveloping them as they ventured deeper. Every snapped twig and rustle of leaves heightened their senses, alert for any sign of their missing friends. The forest felt alive, holding its secrets close, but Jolly and Shawnee were determined to uncover the truth and bring Odin and Challi home.

****

Odin and Challi trekked carefully through the rugged mountains, their horses crunching on the rocky terrain. The air was thin, and a biting wind whipped around them, making the journey feel even more daunting. Scar, the fierce grizzly, who was said to defend his territory with unmatched ferocity. As they climbed higher, the trees thinned out, and the rocky cliffs loomed ominously above them, casting long shadows across the ground.

Suddenly, a low growl echoed through the valley, sending chills down Odin's spine. He exchanged a worried glance with Challi, who tightened his grip on his mare mule. They both knew that Scar was near. The stories had painted him as a monstrous creature, unlike anything they had ever encountered. With every step, they could feel the tension in the air, thickening with the promise of confrontation.

As they rounded a bend, they finally spotted Scar. He was massive, his dark fur blending seamlessly with the shadows of the mountains. His eyes glinted with a predatory intelligence, and he stood poised, ready to defend his territory. Odin felt a surge of adrenaline as he realized they had unwittingly intruded on Scar's domain.

There was no turning back now; they had come too far to retreat.

"Stay calm," Odin whispered, his eyes fixed on the beast. Challi nodded, but his heart raced. They had come not to fight. Slowly, they took a step forward, hands raised to indicate peace. It was a risky move, but they needed Scar to understand their intentions.

Scar charged with fierce determination, his muscles coiling like spring-loaded traps. His eyes were locked onto Odin ready to unleash a blow that could spell disaster for his friend, Challi. In a swift motion, Scar hurled himself between them, the force of his body colliding with the chilling gust of wind that danced through the trees. The impact knocked Challi out of the way, his voice barely a whisper as he called for Odin, fear etched across his features.

As Challi landed heavily in the snow, a cloud of white powder erupted around him, momentarily obscuring his vision. The world seemed to slow, the sounds of the wilderness fading as he focused on the threat before him. Challi, shaken but resilient, pushed himself up from the ground, brushing snow from his brow. He looked around, the cold air biting at his skin, but his eyes remained fixed on his friend—one a protector and the other a foe.

The jagged face of a huge ice wall loomed ominously in the dim twilight of a Dakota day, casting an eerie shadow over the rocky gorge. Challi lay sprawled on the ground, one side of his face smeared with a dried mask of frozen blood, remnants of a struggle that had left him battered and disoriented. The chilling moan of a hideous grizzly bear echoed off the gorge walls, sending a wave of dread through him. With a shudder, Challi opened his eyes, struggling to comprehend his surroundings as the world around him blurred into focus.

Just as the monstrous form of Scar, the bear, loomed over him, a sudden glint of bravery surged through Challi's veins. In the distance, he saw Odin gripping his Henry rifle in his hands. The tension crackled in the frigid air, a silent acknowledgment passing between the two men. As Scar opened its maw, revealing rows of jagged teeth, Odin's resolve hardened. He took aim, the rifle steady against his shoulder, and with a swift movement, he cocked the hammer back.

The shot rang out, echoing like thunder midst the stillness of the gorge. Scar recoiled, its giant dark eyes blinking in surprise as the bullet struck true. Challi, fueled by adrenaline, scrambled to his feet, his heart racing as he felt the weight of the moment settle upon him. He knew he had to move, to act, before the bear regained its composure and turned its wrath upon them. Odin, with steely determination, swung the rifle at the beast, firing again and again, each shot punctuating the beast.

The bear snarled, its fierce growl reverberating through the rocky landscape as Odin's shots rang out.

Each bullet found its mark, and Challi could see the pain etched into Scar's face. The creature staggered back, confusion mingling with rage as it assessed the situation. Challi felt a mix of fear and hope; they had a chance to escape, to survive this encounter if they worked together. The bond between them, forged through countless trials, ignited a glimmer of courage in Challi's heart.

Yet, the grizzly was not easily deterred. With a furious roar, Scar lunged forward, a mass of fur and muscle aimed directly at Odin. Challi's instincts kicked in, and without thinking, he dashed towards his friend, ready to help him defend against the monstrous threat. He could hear Odin shouting commands, urging him to stay back, but Challi could not hold still. Their friendship and trust were the only threads binding them in this moment of terror.

In a blur of motion, Challi reached Odin's side just as the bear charged. Together, they stood firm, their backs to each other, a united front against the beast. Odin continued to fire the rifle, while Challi searched for anything he could use as a weapon. He spotted a jagged piece of ice, sharp and menacing, and grasped it tightly. They were outnumbered by the ferocity of nature, but in that moment, they were resolute—two against the wilderness, fighting for their lives midst the haunting beauty of the Dakota Territory.

Blood dripped down into the snow, the beast was hurting badly. Odin fired yet again at the massive grizzly.

It stumbled back and fell to its death, blood poured out of the numerous wounds that Odin had made.

Odin stood at the edge of the clearing, his heart racing as he watched his friend Challi approach the massive Scar, the beast that had been stalking them for days. Scar was known for his cunning, often playing dead to lure unsuspecting hunters into a false sense of security. "Say, you get away from there," Odin shouted, his voice echoing in the stillness of the forest. He knew the danger all too well, but Challi seemed undeterred, his determination blinding him to the warning signs.

Ignoring Odin's plea, Challi marched forward, his tomahawk gleaming in the dappled sunlight that filtered through the leaves above. Scar lay sprawled on the ground, his fur matted and his breath shallow, but there was an unsettling stillness about him. Challi gripped his weapon tightly, convinced that this time he had finally bested the beast. The thought of glory and victory danced in his mind, drowning out any sense of caution.

With a fierce shout, Challi lunged forward and stabbed Scar several times in the belly. The beast let out a series of grunts, each one a mix of pain and surprise. Odin's eyes widened in horror as he watched the scene unfold. He wanted to scream, to rush in and pull Challi back, but he was rooted to the spot, a mix of fear and disbelief keeping him frozen. The snow-capped forest seemed to hold its breath, the air thick with tension.

As the final blow fell, Scar's body convulsed, his powerful frame shuddering under the onslaught. Challi stood over the beast, panting heavily, a mixture of triumph and adrenaline coursing through his veins. But Odin's instincts screamed that something was wrong. Scar's eyes flickered, an unsettling glint that spoke of a predator not yet defeated. "Challi, stop!" Odin shouted again, but it was too late.

With a final, defiant grunt, Scar's strength surged back. He rolled onto his feet with a speed that belied his apparent wounds, his fangs bared in a snarl. Challi's expression shifted from triumph to terror as he realized his grave mistake. The beast was not dead; it had merely been waiting for the right moment to strike back. Odin could see the panic in Challi's eyes as he stumbled backward, desperately trying to regain his footing.

The forest erupted with the sounds of chaos as Scar lunged at Challi, who barely managed to evade the brutal attack. Odin, now fully alert, grabbed a nearby branch and prepared to defend his friend. The battle was far from over, and as he watched Challi scramble to his feet, he knew that their only chance of survival was to outsmart the beast they had underestimated. Together, they had to find a way to escape the wrath of Scar, the creature that had turned their victory into a nightmare.

Scar, the colossal creature that haunted their nightmares. It was a beast of blood and fury, a killing machine that seemed to emerge from the depths of their darkest fears. When the ground shook beneath their feet, they knew they had to make a choice they had never considered before. In a moment of sheer panic, they did the one thing they never thought to do – run! They sprinted away as fast as their legs could carry them, adrenaline surging through their bodies.

As they dashed through the dense undergrowth, the sound of Scar's massive footsteps echoed behind them. Odin glanced back, his heart pounding in his chest, and saw the beast barreling toward them, its steely frame glinting ominously in the sunlight. He could feel Challi's breath quickening beside him, the fear palpable in the air. They knew they could not outrun it forever, and soon they would have to confront their fate. The landscape around them began to shift as they reached a high cliff, a hanging ledge that seemed to stretch endlessly into the abyss below.

Odin turned to Challi, urgency in his eyes. "We have to get to the ledge!" he shouted, and without waiting for a reply, he shoved him to the side to make room for a desperate leap. The beast was gaining on them, its massive roar drowning out the sound of their racing hearts. In that split second, Odin's mind raced with fearful thoughts. There was no time to think, only to act. He had to save Challi; he had to save himself.

As Scar approached, a massive shadow engulfed him. Odin's instincts kicked in; he dove to the side just in time, narrowly avoiding the beast's crushing charge. The ground trembled violently as Scar collided with the edge of the ledge, its weight too much to bear. Odin watched in horror as the creature lost its balance, teetering precariously over the edge. Time seemed to slow down as the realization dawned on him – this was the end for Scar.

With a resounding crash, the beast plummeted over the side, its massive body twisting and turning as it disappeared into the depths below. A sudden silence enveloped the area, leaving only the sound of Odin and Challi's heavy breathing. They stood there, hearts racing, processing what had just happened. The threat that had loomed over them for so long was gone, but the adrenaline still surged through their veins, leaving them feeling both exhilarated and terrified.

As they looked down into the chasm where Scar had fallen, a strange sense of relief washed over them. They had faced the beast and survived against all odds. Challi turned to Odin, his eyes wide with disbelief. Speaking in Sioux Odin nodded, his mind still racing with what had just transpired. They had escaped the clutches of fear, but they knew that their journey was far from over. Together, they would face whatever challenges lay ahead, bonded by the shared experience of survival and the knowledge that they were stronger than they had ever imagined.

Jolly rode swiftly on Shawnee, his loyal steed, toward the distant Turtle Mountains. The sun hung low in the sky, casting long shadows across the rugged terrain.

Each jolt of Shawnee's gallop sent fresh waves of pain shooting through Jolly's body, reminding him of the wound that had left him bleeding profusely. He grimaced, urging Shawnee to go faster, knowing that time was of the essence. If he could reach Odin's cabin in time, perhaps there was still a chance to heal and recover from this perilous situation.

Chapter 11

As he raced onward, Jolly's thoughts were consumed by the events that had led him to this desperate moment. Just days before, he had been in town, laughing and sharing stories with his friends. But then, the shadow of danger had fallen upon their peaceful lives. Scalp hunters led by Digger and Hawk Grim, wreaking havoc and stealing what little the Sioux had. In an attempt to protect his home, Jolly had confronted them, only to be met with overwhelming force. It had cost him dearly, but he had managed to escape, determined to seek help from Odin.

Shawnee's hooves thundered against the earth as they navigated the winding paths that led toward the mountains. Jolly's vision blurred, and he could feel the warmth of his blood soaking through his clothes. He clutched the reins tightly, fighting to stay conscious. The thought of Challi haunted him. He had been caught in the chaos, and he feared the worst. His resolve strengthened; he had to make it to Brannock's, for his sake as much as his own.

As they neared the foothills of the Turtle Mountains, a strange stillness enveloped the area. The air felt heavy, and the usual sounds of nature seemed muted. Jolly's heart raced, not just from the pain but from an instinctual sense of foreboding. He could see the silhouette of Odin's cabin in the distance, a beacon of hope amidst the encroaching darkness. With a final surge of energy, he urged Shawnee onward, determined to reach the safety of his friend's home.

Upon arriving, Jolly stumbled off Shawnee, collapsing in front of the cabin. Standing at the hitching post, were Thor and Challi's mare mule. Odin emerged, his eyes widening at the sight of Jolly's condition. "Jolly! What happened?" he asked, rushing to Jolly's side. With labored breaths, Jolly recounted the harrowing details of the attack and his desperate need for help. Odin nodded, immediately assessing the wound and moving to gather his medical know how. "You're not too late, but we must act quickly," he said, his voice calm and steady.

With deft hands, Odin worked to clean and dress Jolly's wound, murmuring incantations as he did so. The pain began to ebb, replaced by a soothing coolness as the meds took effect. As Jolly lay there, he felt a sense of peace wash over him, but his mind remained restless. He couldn't shake the worry for Challi. "Gotta warn ya," he urged, but Odin held up a hand. "First, you must heal. You will need your strength." Jolly nodded, understanding.

Challi stepped inside the small cabin, the chill of the outside air clinging to him like a wet blanket. He had been gathering wood for the fireplace, the crisp autumn leaves crunching beneath his feet. As he wiped the sweat from his brow, he noticed Jolly lying in bed, his face pale and strained. A knot of worry twisted in Challi's stomach, and he rushed to his friend's side, speaking in Sioux, his words tumbling out in a mixture of relief and urgency. "I'm so glad you're here," he said, cradling Jolly's head gently in his hands.

Odin was already bent over Jolly, his brow furrowed in concentration. "Be still, Jolly, I can't get the bullet out if you keep squirming," he instructed, the sternness in his voice a stark contrast to the palpable tension in the room. Challi felt a surge of gratitude for Odin's presence; he was always the level-headed one, the one with the skills to mend what was broken.

"Damn, you're worse than any doctor that I ever came across," Jolly grunted, his voice strained as he tried to remain still. Challi could see the pain etched across Jolly's face, and it pierced his heart. He wished there was more he could do, but for now, he could only offer his support, his presence a silent vow that they would get through this together.

Odin's hands moved deftly, working to remove the bullet lodged in Jolly's shoulder. Challi watched with bated breath, every moment seeming to stretch into eternity. The flickering light of the fireplace cast shadows on the walls, dancing in time with the rhythm of their hearts—each thump a reminder of their friendship, of the bond that had brought them to this moment. He felt a swell of hope rising within him.

Finally, with a swift motion, Odin pulled the slug from Jolly's shoulder. The metallic object glinted in the firelight as it landed on the table with a dull thud. Challi let out a breath he didn't realize he had been holding, relief washing over him like a warm wave. "It's done," Odin said, his voice steady, but Challi could see the concern still lingering in his eyes.

Jolly winced but managed a weak smile. "You know, I think I'd rather face a bear than go through that again," he joked, attempting to lighten the mood. Challi chuckled softly, the sound easing the tension that had filled the room moments before. Together, they shared a moment of quiet camaraderie, a reminder that even in the darkest times, friendship could be a healing balm. They had survived this, and as long as they had each other, they would face whatever challenges lay ahead.

Odin looked over at Jolly, his heart pounding in his chest. "Who shot ya?" Odin asked, his voice a mix of anger and concern. Jolly leaned heavily against the door, gasping for breath as he tried to gather his thoughts. The shadows in the corner seemed to creep closer, and the air felt thick with tension.

"It was Benny, that no good son of a skunk, he was the one that shot me," Jolly finally managed to spit out, his voice trembling. Odin clenched his fists, an old rage bubbling to the surface. Benny had never been one to let things go, and now, it seemed, he had crossed a line that would not be easily forgiven. Jolly's eyes darted around the room, as if he expected Benny to come barging in at any moment.

"Odin, I came here to warn ya," Jolly continued, his tone turning grave. "It was Milo who was among the ones that killed young Squirt's mama. Killed him for it too." Odin felt a chill run down his spine. Jolly was right; this was all connected, and they were in deep trouble.

"Well, that's just not the worst of it," Jolly said, his voice dropping to a whisper. "More likely they know your back up here and they're likely coming for ya." Odin's mind raced as he processed the information. He had thought he could return to their hometown, find a sense of peace, but it seemed the past was not finished with him yet. The ghosts of old grudges and betrayals loomed large, ready to engulf him again.

"Jolly, what do we do?" Odin asked, his determination hardening. They needed a plan. They couldn't just sit here waiting for Digger or Hawk to come after them. Jolly shook his head, the pain evident on his face, but there was a spark of resolve in his eyes too. "We need to get outta here. Challi's in danger, and they won't think twice about coming for him too."

Chapter 12

As they stepped outside, the cool air hit them like a slap, a stark contrast to the suffocating atmosphere inside the cabin. Odin scanned the empty outdoors, knowing that every shadow could hold danger. They were in a race against time, and each moment they wasted put Challi further at risk. With Jolly by his side, Odin felt a flicker of hope ignite within him. They might be outnumbered, but they weren't going down without a fight. Together, they would face whatever came their way, determined to protect the boy who deserved a chance at a life free from fear.

Dusty with a keen sense for trouble, cautiously poked his nose out of the cabin door. His ears perked up, twitching at every sound. Jolly stepped outside first. "Nothing to it," he said, waving off Dusty's cautious manner. The sun was shining, and the hills were peaceful. Just as Jolly was about to take another step, a deafening rifle blast shattered the calm. The window behind them exploded with splinters, and a coal oil lamp tipped over, sending flames licking up the edge of Odin's curtain.

Odin with a gruff exterior and a heart of gold, rushed into the room, eyes wide with disbelief. "Nothing to huh," he retorted, his voice laced with sarcasm. The flames crackled hungrily as they climbed higher, fueled by the oil that spilled on the wooden floor. Jolly's bravado vanished, replaced by urgency. "Well, I..." he stammered, realizing that the situation was far from safe.

"Help me get this fire under control!" Odin shouted, springing into action. Without hesitation, Dusty darted around the room, barking frantically, trying to alert everyone to the danger. Jolly quickly grabbed a nearby rug, slamming it down onto the flames, while Odin grabbed a bucket of water from the corner. Together, they worked to douse the fire, splashing water with wild abandon. The flames hissed and sputtered as they met the cold water, but they were not yet defeated.

Just when they thought they had the blaze under control, a voice echoed from outside. "I told you you hadn't heard the last from me!" It was Digger. He stepped into the clearing, his wide-brimmed hat casting a shadow over his smirk. Dusty growled low in his throat, sensing the mischief that Digger brought with him. The fire was dwindling, but the tension in the air was palpable.

Jolly turned to face Digger, his face a mix of anger and relief. "This is your fault! You shot that rifle, didn't you?" Digger chuckled, a glint of mischief in his eyes. "What can I say? I just wanted to stir things up a bit." His flippant attitude only fueled Odin's frustration. "You're lucky you didn't burn the whole place down!" he snapped, wiping sweat from his brow as he surveyed the damage.

As the last of the flames flickered out, the group stood in silence, the weight of the moment settling in. Dusty, tired but still vigilant, sniffed the air, ensuring the danger had passed. Jolly finally broke the silence, a smile creeping back onto his face despite the chaos. "Well, I suppose we should be thankful it wasn't worse," he said, trying to lighten the mood. They all chuckled, knowing that as long as they had each other, they could face whatever trouble Digger brought next.

The sun dipped low in the sky, casting long shadows over the rugged landscape as tension hung thick in the air. Inside the cabin, Odin's eyes darted from the shattered window to the door, where the threat loomed just beyond. Digger's voice cut through the stillness, rough and demanding. "Send the boy out, and we'll go. That's all we want is the boy, you hear?" The sound of his rifle shot echoed, a sharp reminder of the stakes at play. Odin clenched his teeth, feeling the weight of the decision pressing down on him.

"Yeah, I heard you," Odin shot back, his voice low but steady. He could feel his heart racing as he prepared himself for the inevitable conflict. With a quick movement, he broke the window further, shards of glass raining down like tiny stars. He steadied his Henry rifle, the cold metal reassuring in his grip, and aimed it at the encroaching danger. A deep breath steadied his hands as he pulled the trigger, sending a volley of shots into the thickening dusk.

Jolly, a steadfast companion, grinned beneath the brim of his hat, his own rifle at the ready. "Bet you wished you'd stayed in bed, huh Challi?" he called, a hint of mockery in his tone, as he poked his Henry rifle out the window as well. The banter was a thin veil over the tension, a way to mask the fear that lurked beneath their bravado. Challi, the boy caught in the maelstrom of adult conflict, remained silent, his wide eyes darting between the men and the chaos outside.

Each rifle shot was a heartbeat, a reminder of their precarious situation. The cabin, once a sanctuary, had become a battleground. Odin could hear Digger's men shouting outside, their motives clear as they demanded the boy. He glanced at Challi, who stood frozen, the weight of the world resting on his young shoulders. "Stay low," Odin instructed, his voice firm but quiet. Challi nodded, instinctively understanding the gravity of the moment.

Outside, the air was thick with gunpowder and desperation. Digger and his men returned fire, the sound of bullets whizzing past the cabin a chilling reminder of the danger they faced. Odin and Jolly exchanged determined glances, their bond forged in the fires of conflict and unwavering loyalty. They had fought together before, but the stakes felt higher this time. The boy's safety was paramount, and they would do whatever it took to protect him.

As the battle raged on, the cabin felt more like a fortress than ever before. Odin's resolve hardened with each passing moment. He would not surrender Challi to Digger's whims. The world outside may have descended into chaos, but inside the cabin, they would stand firm. With a final, steely determination, Odin prepared to fight, knowing that the bond of brotherhood and the innocence of youth hung in the balance.

Brannock stood behind a crumbling cabin wall, his breath steady as he surveyed the scene before him. Digger, with his bravado, shouted over the din of the distant gunfire, trying to rally the others. "You can't win, Brannock! Just look at the firepower we got out here, there's seven of us!" His voice was saturated with false confidence, an attempt to mask the unease seeping into the group. The sun hung low in the sky, casting long shadows that seemed to stretch and claw at the ground, mirroring the tension that lingered in the air.

Jolly, who had been leaning against a nearby cabin wall, rolled his eyes at Digger's antics. "I'd give a hundred dollars if he'd shut up," he muttered under his breath, though the corners of his mouth twitched with a hint of amusement. Jolly had always been the realist of the trio, his mind sharp and analytical. While Digger reveled in the bravado of numbers, Jolly understood that in this deadly game, it wasn't just about the size of the force; it was about strategy and skill.

Challi stood with his bow in hand, focusing intently on his target a few yards away. Dusty circled around him, barking excitedly as if to encourage Challi. The sun filtered through the trees, casting dappled light on the ground, creating a perfect backdrop.

Challi took a deep breath, steadying his aim. He had been practicing every day, determined to improve his skills. With a swift motion, he nocked an arrow, feeling the familiar tension of the bowstring beneath his fingers. Dusty watched intently, his ears perked up, ready for the action that was about to unfold. Challi's focus sharpened, and he released the arrow with precision.

The arrow soared through the air, striking the target with a satisfying thud. Dusty barked joyfully, bouncing on his paws as if celebrating the successful shot. Challi smiled, feeling a rush of accomplishment. He loved these moments spent with Dusty.

Encouraged by his success, Challi stepped back to take a few more shots. He adjusted his stance and drew back another arrow. Dusty continued to bark, as though he understood the importance of the task at hand. With each arrow released, Challi felt his confidence grow, each strike a testament to his hard work and dedication.

As the battle continued, rifle shots after rifle shots were fired. Dusty continued to bark. Challi chuckled, amused by his friend's antics, but he remained focused. He knew that his training was crucial. With the sun beginning to set, casting long shadows across the ground,

Odin and Jolly were too busy to notice Challi had ran out of arrows, and was determined to help out his friends. He took a moment to appreciate the bond he shared with Dusty, the way they complemented each other; two companions on a journey of friendship. With one final shot, Challi aimed carefully, released the arrow, and watched it hit the target once more. Dusty barked, a triumphant sound that echoed through the forest.

As Challi stood tall and defiant on the scarred battlefield, his heart pounding like a war drum. The acrid smell of gunpowder filled the air, mingling with the cries of the wounded and the distant rumble of cannon fire. He let out a war cry that echoed across the chaos, a rallying cry for his comrades. With steely resolve, he ran outside, leaped onto a horse that had miraculously survived the fray. Its coat was matted and dirty, but in that moment, it felt like a trusted companion ready to charge into the fray.

As he settled into the saddle, Challi's eyes blazed with fierce determination. He kicked the horse's ribs, urging it forward, but the creature seemed to have a mind of its own. It stood stubbornly, unmoved by the chaos surrounding them. Challi could hear the crack of rifle shots ringing out, the bullets whizzing dangerously close, yet all he felt was the pulse of adrenaline coursing through his veins. The horse snorted and stamped its hooves, as if sensing the gravity of the moment, but it remained rooted to the spot.

"Challi? What's that fool kid doing?" asked Odin, scratching his head in confusion. His brow furrowed, a mix of concern and annoyance etched on his face. Odin always thinking twice before stepping into the unknown. He had a knack for keeping their small group grounded, often pulling them back from the brink of recklessness.

"Probably skinning out, and I don't blame him," said Jolly with a chuckle, leaning against a cabin wall. With a twinkle in his eye, he had a way of making even the most mundane activities seem exciting. He waved a hand dismissively, as if to brush off Odin's worry.

Frustration bubbled within Challi as he glanced around, taking in the sight of his enemy. He had to act. This was not just a battle; it was a fight for survival. With a fierce tug of the reins and a shout of encouragement, he pleaded with the mule to move. The beast seemed to consider its options, its ears flicking back and forth, attuned to the sounds of chaos that surrounded them.

Just then, a volley of gunfire erupted, and the mule finally responded, as if spurred by instinct rather than command. It leaped forward, galloping into the fray, Challi clinging on tightly as they charged toward the enemy lines. The wind whipped through his hair, and for a moment, he felt invincible. They wove through the chaos, dodging between debris, pushing forward with a single-minded determination. His heart raced, not just from fear, but from the thrill of the charge.

As they closed in on the enemy, Challi's resolve hardened. He could see the fear in their eyes as they realized they were being charged by a lone warrior on horseback. With a fierce shout, he brandished his weapon, his voice rising above the cacophony. The horse beneath him seemed to sense the tide turning, its powerful legs propelling them forward as if fueled by Challi's indomitable spirit. They crashed into the enemy lines, a whirlwind of chaos and defiance.

But in the frenzy of battle, Challi soon discovered that the horse, once obedient, had its own will. As they crashed into the ranks of the enemy, it veered sharply, throwing Challi off balance. He tumbled from the saddle, landing hard on the ground. Dazed, he looked up just in time to see the horse galloping away, leaving him amidst the chaos. Alone, surrounded by the enemy, Challi's heart sank. Yet, even in that moment of vulnerability, he refused to yield. Rising to his feet, he drew his weapon, ready to face whatever came next. The battle was far from over, and Challi would fight until his last breath.

Dusty was sitting quietly in the cabin, the sun filtering through the trees outside, painting patterns on the wooden floor. The tranquility was shattered when he heard a scuffle outside. His heart raced as he realized something was wrong. Challi, his friend, was out there, and the sound of a struggle sent a chill down his spine. Dusty felt a sudden spark of urgency, an instinct that told him he needed to act fast.

As he burst through the cabin door, Dusty's eyes widened at the sight before him. Hawk stood menacingly over Challi, his pistol raised and ready to fire. Time seemed to slow down as Dusty processed the scene. The air was thick with tension, and he could feel the weight of the moment pressing down on him. Without thinking, he charged forward, driven by a mix of fear and determination.

With a powerful shove, Dusty tackled Hawk to the ground, the impact sending shockwaves through both of them. Dusty's paws grasped at Hawk's clothing, pulling and tugging as he fought to disarm him. Hawk, caught off guard, struggled against the sudden onslaught, but Dusty's resolve was unyielding. He knew he had to protect Challi, no matter the cost. The world around them faded away, leaving only the two of them in a desperate struggle.

Chapter 13

Challi, momentarily stunned by the chaos, quickly regained her senses. He scrambled to his feet, his eyes darting between Dusty and Hawk. Speaking in Sioux, he yelled, urgency lacing his voice. The warning echoed in Dusty's mind as he wrestled with Hawk, feeling the man's strength and desperation to reclaim control. The sounds of the forest faded into the background, replaced by the rapid thumping of his heart.

As Dusty fought, he could feel Hawk's grip loosening slightly. The adrenaline coursing through him gave him the strength he needed. With a final push, he managed to knock the pistol from Hawk's hand, sending it skittering across the ground. Hawk, now disarmed, growled in frustration, but Dusty didn't let up. He pinned Hawk down, his chest heaving as he caught his breath, relief flooding through him as he glanced back at Challi.

Hawk struggled against the coyote's fierce grip, the animal's teeth bared in a snarl as it pinned him to the ground. "Digger! Get him off me!" he shouted, panic lacing his voice. The coyote was relentless, its wild instincts driving it to hold on tightly, refusing to let go. Hawk could feel the warmth of the creature's breath, its wild eyes filled with a primal rage. Every second felt like an eternity as he fought to break free from its jaws.

Digger heard the desperation in Hawk's voice. With sharp focus, he turned his rifle toward the tussle. The tension in the air crackled as he steadied his aim. "Hold on, Hawk! I'm coming!" He squeezed the trigger, the sharp report of the gun echoing through the mountains. The bullet found its mark, striking the coyote in its side. The coyote yelped in pain, its grip loosening just enough for Hawk to wriggle free.

As Hawk scrambled to his feet, he glanced at Digger, who was already reloading his rifle, eyes scanning the area for any further threats. The wounded coyote staggered back, its eyes now filled with a mix of fury and confusion. Hawk's heart raced as he regained his breath, adrenaline still coursing through his veins.

The coyote, wounded but not defeated, let out a low growl before retreating into the underbrush, a shadow disappearing into the wild. Hawk and Digger exchanged a look of relief, knowing they had narrowly escaped a grim fate. "You think you can kill that brat, without any more eruptions?" Digger grumbled, his voice a low rumble that echoed off the trees. They moved cautiously, aware that danger could be lurking just beyond the next tree. Together, they navigated the rugged terrain, each step a reminder of how quickly things could change in the wild.

Challi stood in the middle of the clearing, his heart pounding in his chest as he yelled for Dusty. The sun hung low in the sky, casting long shadows that danced around her. Dusty had been involved in a fierce scuffle with Hawk, and now his absence filled the air with an unsettling silence. Speaking in Sioux he called again, his voice echoing off the trees. But there was no response, only the rustling of leaves and the distant chirping of birds.

As he scanned the area, a sharp pain shot through his arm, reminding him of the danger still lurking nearby. The fight had been reckless, and now Dusty was nowhere to be found. Little did he know, he had limped off to a hidden spot to lick his wounds, exhausted and defeated. Meanwhile, Odin, who had witnessed the entire ordeal from a distance, felt a surge of panic. He had always admired Challi's courage, but this time he feared it might lead his to her doom.

Without a second thought, Odin dashed toward the clearing, his legs pumping hard against the ground. He could see Challi's silhouette growing smaller as she moved deeper into the woods, calling for a creature that might not return. "Challi, wait!" he shouted, his voice strained with urgency. He knew he had to reach her before the shadows of the forest swallowed her whole. Each step felt heavier, the weight of his concern dragging him down, but he pressed on, determined to save her.

Finally, he spotted him, standing alone beneath the twisted branches of an ancient tree. Just as he arrived, a low growl echoed through the air, sending chills down his spine. Challi turned, wide-eyed, as a menacing figure emerged from the underbrush. Odin's heart raced as he stepped forward, ready to confront the threat that loomed over them. "Stay back!" he shouted, positioning himself between Challi and the danger. It was a tense moment, the air thick with anticipation as they faced the unknown together, united in their fight for survival.

The tension in the air was palpable as Hawk faced off against Challi. Hawk grinned menacingly, his fingers twitching near the Colt Navy pistol strapped to his hip. "I got you now, kid," he sneered, pulling back the hammer with a satisfying click. The sun glared down on them, illuminating the dirt and sweat that clung to their skin.

Just as Hawk was about to pull the trigger, a sharp crack echoed through the prairie. Jolly had raised his Henry rifle and fired. The bullet struck Hawk square in the chest. Time seemed to freeze as Hawk's expression shifted from triumph to shock. His pistol clattered to the ground as he staggered back, clutching at his shirt, which now blossomed with a dark crimson stain.

Jolly, who had been watching the standoff from the cabin, rushed into the fray. He had seen enough bloodshed in his time and was determined to prevent any more. "Challi! Get back!" he shouted, his voice booming. Jolly shadowed his steely gaze. He approached Hawk cautiously, ready to kill him again, but the sight of the dead scalp hunter made him hesitate.

Jolly walked slowly over to the body of Hawk. The scene before him was grim; Hawk lay lifeless. As he knelt beside his fallen foe. But just as he reached out to touch Hawk's shoulder, a sharp pain pierced through his back, catching him off guard. He gasped, instinctively looking down, and horrified to see blood seeping through his shirt. Panic surged through Jolly as he stumbled back, clutching the wound.

The world around him blurred, the sounds of the night fading into a dull roar. Who had shot him? The realization that he was not alone, that the danger was still lurking in the shadows, brought a wave of adrenaline. He glanced around, searching for the unknown shooter, feeling the cold grip of fear tighten around him. The darkness seemed to close in, and every rustle of leaves felt like a threat.

With a grimace, Jolly forced himself to stand, his body protesting with every movement. He knew he needed to escape, to find cover and tend to his wound, but the weight of Hawk's lifeless form anchored him to the spot. He took a deep breath, steeling himself against the pain, and began to back away slowly, eyes scanning the area for any sign of movement. The moonlight cast eerie shadows, distorting the landscape and making it harder to discern friend from foe.

Chapter 14

Suddenly, a figure emerged from the trees, cloaked in shadow. Jolly's heart raced as he instinctively reached for his weapon, but his strength was waning. He couldn't let the shooter get away; Hawk deserved justice. With what little energy he had left, Jolly summoned his resolve, ready to confront the unknown figure. As the silhouette stepped into the light, Jolly's breath caught in his throat. It was Digger, Hawk's brother. Digger fired again, causing Jolly to topple over blood spewing.

Jolly tried to stand up but it was no use; the rifle wounds were too great. He fell back to his knees, the cold, hard ground pressing against his skin, the pain radiating through him like a wild fire. He grasped at the dirt, fingers clawing for purchase, but his strength was fading. Each breath felt like a weight on his chest, and the world around him blurred into a haze of muted colors and distant sounds. He could hear the echoes of battle in the background, the shouts of men and the sharp cracks of gunfire, but they seemed so far away, like a dream he couldn't quite remember.

Digger stood in the frosty clearing, the sun beating down on him as he cocked the hammer back on his Henry rifle. The weight of the weapon felt familiar in his hands, a tool that had served him well in the past. He was ready to settle a score, the tension in the air thickening with the promise of confrontation. But just as he prepared to take aim, a shadow swooped down from above. It was Odin, a force of nature with a fury that could rival a storm.

Odin tackled Digger, their bodies colliding with a thud that reverberated through the quiet landscape. The rifle clattered to the ground, forgotten for the moment as Odin's rage took control. "This is for what you did to Dusty!" he shouted, the weight of his words punctuated by another slam of Digger's body against the earth. Dusty had been his trustworthy canine for years ever since he rescued him as a pup, a victim of Digger's reckless choices, and Odin was determined to make him pay.

With each slam, Odin's anger fueled his strength. "And this is for what you did to Jolly!" he exclaimed, the name echoing like a haunting melody of loss. Jolly, another casualty of Digger's actions, had been caught in the crossfire of their violent world. Digger, struggling beneath Odin's weight, felt the air leave his lungs with each impact. He had underestimated Odin's resolve, and now, it seemed, he was at the mercy of a man who had lost too much. The ground beneath him felt hard and unyielding, a stark contrast to the warmth of the sun above. He realized that he had pushed Odin too far, and the consequences of his actions were now crashing down upon him.

With a sudden shift in momentum, Odin managed to flip Digger overhead, the world spinning for a brief moment before Digger hit the ground again with a resounding thud. The pain shot through him, sharp and unforgiving. He lay there, breathless and stunned, staring up at the sky as he tried to reconcile the gravity of the situation. This was not just a fight; it was an reckoning, a moment where the past collided violently with the present.

As Digger struggled to regain his composure, he realized that he could no longer escape the ghosts of his past. Dusty and Jolly would not be forgotten, and neither would the pain inflicted upon their loved ones. In that moment of vulnerability, he understood that the battle was not just physical; it was a fight for redemption, a chance to confront the consequences of his choices. With Odin standing over him, ready to deliver more punishment, Digger knew that it was time to face the music.

Jolly lay on the ground, his body battered and bruised, struggling to catch his breath. The chaos around him blurred into a haze of movement and noise as he watched Odin and Digger grapple for control over the prized Henry rifle. It was a weapon that had seen many battles, and now it was the focus of their fierce rivalry. Jolly lifted himself onto one elbow, squinting through the dust and the pain, trying to comprehend the scuffle that unfolded before him.

Odin pushed against Digger, who was smaller but fierce. Just as Odin seemed to gain the upper hand,

Digger retaliated with a swift knee to Odin's gut. The air whooshed out of Odin as he doubled over, and Digger seized the moment to spin around and deliver a powerful kick to Odin's head. The force of the blow sent Odin crashing to the ground, landing hard just inches away from Jolly, who felt a mix of pity and relief wash over him.

As Jolly's heart raced, he realized that the rifle was still within reach, lying a short distance from where Odin had fallen. With every ounce of strength he could muster, Jolly crawled toward the weapon, ignoring the burning pain in his limbs. Digger, sensing Jolly's movement, turned to see him reaching for the rifle. The desperation in Jolly's eyes fueled Digger's aggression, and he lunged forward, determined to claim the weapon for himself.

In that moment, as the two of them struggled to get their hands on the Henry rifle, a realization struck Jolly. Their fight was not just about the rifle; it was a fight for survival, for power, and for respect in this unforgiving world. The realization bolstered his resolve. He summoned every bit of energy left in him and, with a last push, grasped the rifle. The moment their hands met on the cold metal, the fight shifted, and the air around them crackled with tension, as the three of them found themselves at a crossroads, each considering what they would do next.

Jolly stood by, watching as Digger and Odin struggled over a gleaming Henry rifle. The weapon gleamed in the waning light, a symbol of power and danger, and the two men wrestled with it as if it were a wild beast.

"Let go, Digger!" Odin shouted, his voice tinged with a mix of excitement and fear. The rifle jerked violently between them, each man refusing to yield, their faces flushed with effort. Jolly, sensing the tension mounting, felt a jolt of instinctive concern. He knew that the rifle was not just a toy; it was a tool that could bring harm if not handled properly. The air crackled with unspoken danger, and Jolly's heart raced as he thought of how their antics might end.

In a moment of impulsive bravery, Jolly decided he could not stand idly by. He leaped forward, his intention to intervene clear in his eyes. "Let me—" But before he could finish his thought, the rifle slipped from their grasp, and instinct took over. Jolly hurled himself into the fray, determined to shield his friend from what he feared would be a catastrophe. Time seemed to slow as he threw himself in front of the rifle, hoping to disarm the situation.

The world around him erupted in a deafening bang as the rifle discharged. Jolly felt a searing pain as the bullet struck him in the chest. He grimaced, the shock coursing through his body, the warmth of blood spreading across his shirt like a dark bloom. Digger and Odin froze, their faces transforming from confusion to horror as they realized what had just happened.

"Damn it, Jolly!" Odin shouted, rushing to his side. His hands trembled as he assessed the wound, panic flashing in his eyes. Odin knelt beside him, his usual bravado stripped away, replaced by a look of genuine fear. "What were you thinking?" he stammered, his voice shaking. Jolly winced but managed a weak grin, trying to ease the tension. "Just thought I'd take the bullet for you," he joked, though the pain made it hard to keep the humor alive.

Digger stood in the clearing, feeling the weight of the rifle in his hands. The metallic scent of gun oil mixed with the earthy aroma of the surrounding forest. He had come out here for some quiet time, but the tranquility was swiftly shattered when the rifle slipped from his grip and clattered to the ground. He bent down to retrieve it, feeling the cool steel against his palm as he cocked the hammer back, ready to defend himself against whatever threat might emerge.

Just as he steadied himself, a sudden rustling erupted from the underbrush. Digger's heart raced as he prepared to face whatever danger lurked in the shadows. To his surprise, it was Dusty who burst through the foliage. Dusty was limping, a gash on his side oozing blood, but despite his injury, he charged forward with the determination of a warrior. In an unexpected twist of fate, Dusty tackled Digger to the ground, his teeth gripping the fabric of Digger's shirt, ripping it to shreds.

"Help! Get this mangy coyote off me!" Digger yelled. The weight of Dusty, though small compared to Digger, pinned him down momentarily. Digger kicked and screamed hoping to get Odin's attention to pull him off of him. Dusty's loyalty was fierce, and he seemed to sense Digger was a threat. Digger managed to wriggle out from under Dusty's grasp, and he sat up, brushing leaves and dirt off his clothes while glancing around for any sign of danger. He kicked the animal hard in the side. He yelped again.

Digger confronted Dusty, the coyote that had been a thorn in his side. With a swift motion, he swung the rifle's butt end, the sound of wood against flesh echoing through the stillness. "Damn, coyote, that'll teach ya," Digger spat, his voice full of anger. Dusty yelped, recoiling from the unexpected blow, but his fierce bark soon filled the air again, warning of an impending danger lurking nearby.

Odin, who had been observing from a distance, felt a surge of protectiveness for his friend Jolly, who lay injured on the ground. He pulled out his Colt Navy pistol, the weight of it familiar and comforting in his hands. With deliberate calm, he cocked the hammer back, knowing he had to act quickly. Digger turned at just the right moment, but it was too late. Odin fired twice, the sharp reports of the gun shattering the quiet, and Digger fell to his knees, his defiance extinguished like a candle in the wind.

As Digger's lifeless form crumpled to the ground, the remaining men who had once stood beside him dropped their weapons in fear, their courage evaporating like morning mist. They mounted their horses and rode away, leaving the scene in a cloud of dust and uncertainty. Dusty, still on high alert, continued to bark and growl, his instincts warning of something more than just the danger that had just passed. Something was amiss in the underbrush, and Odin could feel it too.

Turning his attention back to Jolly, Odin knelt beside his friend, who lay gasping, his life slipping away like sand through fingers. Jolly flickered his eyes, a final attempt to convey the bond they shared, but it was no use. With a last, shuddering breath, Jolly passed on, leaving Odin with a heavy heart and a sorrow that felt unbearable. He hung his head low, a silent tribute to the man who had stood by him through thick and thin.

With the weight of loss resting on his shoulders, Odin stood up fully, rifle at the ready. He scanned the area, the sun filtering through the leaves, casting dappled shadows that danced around him. The scene was serene, yet the joy of nature felt muted, overshadowed by the grief of losing a dear friend. Dusty, sensing Odin's turmoil, looked back toward the bushes, growling softly as if urging him to be cautious.

Odin took a step forward into the thickening gloom, aware that danger could still linger. The silence felt oppressive, and he wondered if he would have to face more than just the shadows of his past. With each careful footfall, he kept his eyes peeled for any sign of movement, knowing that the world had changed in an instant. The bond between man and beast was strong, and with Dusty by his side, he vowed to honor Jolly's memory, ready to confront whatever darkness lay ahead.

In the deep silence of the forest, the rustling of leaves stirred a sense of dread in Odin's heart. He crouched low, his Henry rifle gripped firmly in his hands, eyes scanning the underbrush for any signs of movement. The scalp hunters had been ruthless, and the memory of their savagery lingered like a dark cloud over the camp. Just as he was about to pull the trigger, a figure burst forth from the thicket. It was Challi, his face marked with urgency and fear.

Odin's tension eased slightly, but his mind raced as he noticed the limp form of Dusty sprawled on the ground nearby. Challi dashed over, kneeling beside Dusty, who was gravely wounded. The sight of his friend in such distress struck a blow to Odin's heart. Dusty's breaths were shallow, and a dark stain spread across his fur, a stark contrast against the green of the forest floor. Challi's hands trembled as he began to pray in Sioux, his words flowing like a river of hope into the stillness of the air.

Time slipped away as Challi poured his energy into the prayer, his voice rising and falling like the wind through the trees. Odin watched, a mix of admiration and helplessness churning within him. Minutes stretched into hours, the sun arching across the sky, its light flickering through the branches above. The forest, once vibrant with life, felt eerily quiet, as if holding its breath in anticipation of Dusty's fate.

Finally, as the last rays of sunlight began to fade, Challi raised his head from the ground, a weary look etched on his face. His eyes searched for Jolly, who had been on watch not far from their cabin. The silence that followed was heavy with unspoken fears. Odin, knowing what had to be said, lowered his head, the weight of his words pressing against his chest. "He's gone, Challi," Odin said softly, his voice barely breaking the stillness.

A moment of silence passed, as the stark reality of their situation settled in. Challi's face twisted in grief, the prayer still lingering on his lips, now mingling with sorrow. Dusty's life hung by a thread, and Jolly's absence left a void that could not be filled. The forest around them seemed to echo their loss, each rustle of leaves a reminder of the fragility of life within it.

Odin felt a surge of determination amid the despair. They could not allow Jolly's sacrifice to be in vain. He reached out a hand, placing it on Challi's shoulder, offering strength in the face of overwhelming grief. Together, they would honor their fallen friend, and reclaim the peace that the scalp hunters had stolen from them. The forest, though dark and threatening, was still their home, and they would fight to protect it, for Jolly, for Dusty, and for each other.

Challi knelt beside Dusty, his heart heavy with sadness. The once vibrant fur of his beloved companion lay matted and dusty against the ground, a stark reminder of the battle they had just endured. Challi gently stroked Dusty's fur, whispering soft words of love and encouragement. "You're going to be okay, buddy," he murmured in Sioux, hoping that his touch would somehow convey the warmth and strength he wished to share. Dusty remained still, his eyes closed, a peaceful facade that Challi feared masked the truth of his condition.

As Challi's fingers brushed against Dusty's fur, he felt a surge of protectiveness rise within him. The bond they shared was deeper than any words could express. He remembered all the adventures they had gone on together, the laughter and joy that filled their days. But now, reality loomed like a dark cloud. Challi turned his gaze upward to Odin, whose expression mirrored the turmoil in Challi's heart. Odin's eyes were glassy, reflecting the weight of unshed tears, and Challi could see the conflict brewing within him.

"I promised Jolly I'd turn you over to your people, and that's what I'm gonna do," Odin said, his voice steady but burdened. The words hung in the air, thick and heavy. Challi understood Odin's duty, yet a pang of fear gripped him. He didn't want to lose Dusty—not like this.

He wanted to fight for his friend, to find a way to heal him before any decisions were made. But the reality of their situation left Challi feeling powerless, trapped in a moment he wished he could change.

Slowly, Challi turned back to Dusty. The sight of his friend lying there, seemingly lifeless, made his heart ache. Dusty had always been the brave one, the protector, and now he looked so vulnerable. Challi leaned down, pressing his forehead against Dusty's. "I won't leave you, not now," he whispered, feeling the warmth of Dusty's body beneath him. It was a flicker of hope—a reminder that Dusty was still there, even if he seemed far away.

Challi's mind raced with thoughts of what could be done. He thought of the healers in his village, the remedies they had used before, and the stories of recovery that filled his heart with determination. Dusty was not just a pet; he was family, and Challi would do anything to ensure his safety. He looked back at Odin, desperation edging into his voice. Speaking again in Sioux.

Odin's expression softened as he took in Challi's fervor. He stepped closer, kneeling beside them. "You're right, Challi. Dusty is special, and we owe it to him to try." A newfound resolve sparked between them, as the shadows of despair began to lift. Together, they would search for the answers they needed, for Dusty's sake and for their own. Hope blossomed anew in the air around them, and as they worked together, they realized that love and friendship could conquer even the darkest of times.

Odin stood with his brow furrowed with concern as he looked down at Dusty, the large, coyote who was lying still on the ground. Dusty was a loyal companion. Challi, Odin's friend, hurried over, his face a mix of worry and determination. "Help me get him up and into the cabin," said Odin, his voice steady but urgent.

Challi nodded, and together they knelt beside Dusty. With careful hands, they each grabbed hold of his paws. Dusty looked up at them with his big, sad eyes, as if he understood their intentions. With a gentle heave, they lifted him up, feeling the weight of his body as they maneuvered him to stand. Dusty let out a soft whine, but he managed to find his footing, leaning into them for support.

As they began to walk, Dusty's legs wobbled slightly, but Odin and Challi steadied him. They took slow, measured steps, their hearts pounding with the effort and the worry that hung in the air. The cabin was not far, but with Dusty's weight and his unsteady state, every step felt like a small victory. Challi whispered words of encouragement to Dusty, hoping to inspire him to keep going.

The cabin, an old wooden structure nestled among the trees, finally came into view. Its welcoming presence was a comfort to both Odin and Challi. They pushed through the door, and the warm air enveloped them, contrasting the cool breeze outside. With a final push, they managed to get Dusty inside, where he immediately flopped down on the soft rug in front of the fireplace.

Odin sighed with relief as he knelt beside Dusty, gently patting his head. "You're going to be okay, buddy," he reassured him. Challi went to fetch a bowl of water, wanting to make sure Dusty was hydrated. As he returned, he noticed Dusty's breathing had calmed, and his tail gave a weak thump against the floor.

They settled down around Dusty, keeping a watchful eye on him. The crackling of the fire filled the silence, and soon Dusty started to perk up, his eyes shining with gratitude. Odin and Challi exchanged glances, knowing they had done the right thing. Together, they would ensure that Dusty was cared for, and that the bond they shared would only grow stronger in the warmth of friendship and love.

The sudden bark from Dusty had startled him, a deep, throaty sound that echoed through the still afternoon. "You scared me half to death!" he exclaimed, shaking his head in disbelief. Dusty with an infectious spirit, had been lying quietly just moments before, but now he was bouncing around, his tail wagging furiously as if he hadn't just sent Odin's heart into a frenzy.

****

Odin woke up to the soft light filtering through the cabin's windows, casting gentle shadows across the wooden floor. He stretched, feeling the muscles in his arms and back loosen as the warmth of the sun began to embrace him. Today was significant; it marked the day Challi would meet his people, the Sioux. The thought stirred a mix of excitement and nervousness within him. He knew how much this moment meant to him, and he wanted it to be perfect.

He turned towards the small bed in the corner where Challi lay sleeping. His long, dark hair fanned out across the pillow, and his face was peaceful, lips slightly parted as he breathed in the tranquility of the morning. Odin approached quietly, kneeling beside him. "Challi," he whispered gently, brushing a loose strand of hair away from his face. "It's time to wake up." He watched as his eyelids fluttered open, revealing his bright, curious eyes. A smile broke across his face as he realized today was finally here.

Challi sat up, rubbing the sleep from his eyes. Challi spoke in Sioux and then Odin nodded, and he quickly sprang from the bed, his excitement palpable. "I can't believe I'm finally going to meet them! My people!" spoken in Sioux as Challi exclaimed, his heart racing with anticipation. Odin felt a swell of pride for him; he had seen how hard he had worked to connect with his Sioux heritage, learning their traditions and stories.

As they prepared for the day, Odin and Challi shared a simple breakfast of fruits and bread. The cabin, filled with the aroma of fresh food, felt warm and inviting. "I hope they accept me," Challi said in Sioux, his voice tinged with uncertainty. Odin reached across the table, taking his hand in his. "You have their blood in you, Challi. They will see the strength and spirit that you carry. Just be yourself." Challi nodded, taking comfort in his words, though the flutter in his stomach remained.

Odin, Challi, and Dusty gathered around the breakfast table, the last remnants of their meal still lingering on their plates. The sun peeked through the window, casting a warm glow over the rustic wooden room. Dusty bounced around on the cabin floor, excitement radiating from him like the morning light. Challi spoke in Sioux. Odin grin spreading across his face. "Yes, we are! It's going to be an adventure!"

After clearing the table, the three friends hurried to gather their supplies. Odin took charge, stuffing their saddlebags with essentials: a canteen, beef jerky, a map, and a compass. Dusty, barely able to contain his energy, dashed around the room, ensuring they didn't forget anything. Challi kept a watchful eye, making sure they had enough food for the journey ahead. With their bags packed and hearts full of excitement, they set out towards the Montana Territory, the promise of adventure beckoning them.

The trail they chose was lined with towering pine trees, their fragrance filling the air as they walked. Dusty led the way, his little legs working hard to keep up with Odin and Challi. The path wound through the forest, and every now and then, they would stop to marvel at the wildlife around them. A deer peeked out from behind a bush, and Dusty squealed with delight. Challi smiled, enjoying the simple beauty of nature, while Odin took a moment to capture the scene in his mind, knowing it would be a memory to treasure.

As they ventured deeper into the territory, the landscape began to change. The trees grew sparse, and the ground became rocky. Dusty, undeterred by the obstacles, climbed over the stones with determination. Challi occasionally paused to help him, his gentle nature shining through as he encouraged him to keep going. Odin, ever the protector, took the lead, ensuring that they stayed on the right path. He pointed toward the distant mountains, their peaks dusted with snow, and said, "That's where we're heading. We'll find the best view up there!"

The trio continued their trek, the sun shifting in the sky, casting long shadows behind them. As they climbed higher, they could feel the cool mountain air brushing against their cheeks. Dusty, now a little tired but still enthusiastic. The bond between the three friends strengthened with each step, their laughter echoing in the open space around them.

Finally, they reached a clearing at the mountain's edge, revealing a breathtaking view of the valley below. The sight took their breath away, and for a moment, they stood in silence, taking it all in. Odin, Challi, and Dusty had made it, and the world stretched out before them like a beautiful painting. Dusty jumped up and down, filled with joy. Challi and Odin exchanged proud smiles.

A Sioux camp, a short walk through the vibrant green woods. The air was fresh, filled with the sounds of chirping birds and rustling leaves. As they walked, Odin shared stories about the Sioux way of life, the importance of nature, and the bonds of community. Challi listened intently, absorbing every word, his heart swelling with pride for the culture he was about to embrace fully.

When they finally arrived at the camp, the sight took Challi's breath away. The large, beautifully decorated tipis dotted the landscape, and the laughter and chatter of people filled the air. Children ran freely, their joyful shouts echoing through the trees. Odin squeezed his hand reassuringly, and together they stepped into the circle of his heritage, ready to begin a new chapter in his life. The journey ahead was unknown, but Challi felt a sense of belonging that he had longed for, and with Odin by his side, he was ready to face whatever came next.

In the quiet valley nestled between the granite walls of the Mission Mountains and the towering peaks of the Swan Range, the trio prepared for an adventure. Odin, Challi and Dusty had grown up in this picturesque landscape, where the mountains seemed to touch the sky and the snow-capped their majestic tops throughout the year. They often spent their weekends exploring the lush forests that blanketed the valley, but today they decided to venture higher, seeking the thrill of the trails that wound along the foothills.

As they rode, the air was crisp and fresh, filling their lungs with the scent of pine and earth. Odin led the way, pointing out various plants and animals along the trail. Little Bird, Tantrum, Quickstrike were amazed to see Challi. They hadn't known any other Sioux before. Tantrum and Quickstrike, ever the jokesters, entertained the group with silly stories and laughter that echoed against the granite walls, creating an atmosphere of joy and camaraderie.

The ride was not without its challenges; steep inclines made them work hard, and the rocky terrain required careful footing. However, the breathtaking views kept their spirits high. As they reached a particularly high vantage point, they paused to take in the sprawling valley below. The sun began to dip towards the horizon, casting a golden hue over the snow-capped peaks, creating a scene that felt almost magical. They stood together, united by the beauty of their surroundings, each lost in their thoughts, but feeling connected by the moment.

As the day turned to dusk, the temperature dropped, and Odin and Dusty decided it was time to head back. They retraced their steps, the laughter still ringing in the air, though now mixed with a sense of calm as the stars began to shimmer above. The granite walls of the Mission Mountains and the Swan Range stood tall and proud, guardians of their memories. It was a day well spent, one that would be etched in their hearts as they continued to explore the wonders of their valley, always finding new adventures just beyond the next rise.

The sun dipped low on the horizon, casting a warm golden hue over the Great Plains as Odin and Dusty prepared to leave the Sioux camp. They had come to learn and share stories, but now, as they stood before Chall an untamed spirit, a heavy weight settled in their hearts. Challi's small hands clutched a feathered necklace; a gift from Odin, symbolizing friendship and understanding. The air was thick with unspoken words, and Challi's innocent confusion mirrored the tension of a world divided.

"No, Challi, no, this is your family now. You have to stay here now," Odin said, his voice gentle yet firm. The words hung in the air like the last notes of a haunting melody, resonating against the backdrop of distant mountains. Dusty shifted uneasily, his gaze drifting over the camp, where laughter of the Sioux children intertwined with the distant calls of nature. He wished fervently that they could bridge the chasm that separated their worlds, but deep down, he understood the impossibility of it all.

Challi's face fell, shadows creeping into the corners of his smile. Once again, Challi spoke in Sioux he pleaded, his voice a mix of hope and desperation. The Sioux way was woven into every fiber of his being, yet the allure of the two outsiders ignited a spark of adventure within him. He dreamed of exploring beyond the plains, of traveling to faraway lands where the sun set differently and the rivers sang new songs.

Odin knelt down, meeting Challi's gaze with a sincerity that belied their cultural divide. "We would love to stay, Challi. Your people have shown us kindness that we will carry forever. But our lives are different, and we have to go back." He felt the weight of his words, knowing they offered little comfort. The stark reality was that the fabric of their societies was woven with threads of misunderstanding and conflict, a tapestry that seemed impossible to untangle.

Challi's voice trembled, his youthful innocence clashing with the harshness of reality. Odin exchanged a glance with Dusty, their hearts aching for the boy who saw the world with such clarity. Challi's wisdom, so profound yet unrecognized, danced on the edges of their thoughts, igniting a flicker of hope that perhaps one day, barriers could dissolve like morning mist.

As dusk settled in, painting the sky with hues of lavender and indigo, Odin placed a hand on Challi's shoulder, grounding him in the moment. "One day, young one, the world will learn to dance together, just like the stars. But until then, carry our stories with you. We will always be a part of you, just as you will be a part of us." With that, they embraced, an exchange of warmth and understanding that transcended language or lineage.

In that fleeting moment, a bridge was forged, a glimmer of possibility amidst a turbulent reality, illuminating the path for future generations who dared to dream of unity.

Challi stood at the edge of the Sioux camp, the sun dipping low in the sky, casting long shadows across the ground. He watched his friends leave, the dust swirling beneath the hooves of their horses. Among them was Shawnee, tied to the mare mule with a rope that felt heavier than it should have. Odin, ever the stoic one, pulled the mule along, his expression unreadable. As they departed, he turned back to Challi and said, "Jolly would want you to have this. To remember him by." The weight of those words lingered in the air, heavy with unsaid emotions.

With a bittersweet pang in his chest, Challi shook his head. Jolly was gone. He stepped into the stirrups of his blue roan horse, a creature as wild as the spirit of the plains themselves. As he released the mare mule into the wild, the animal trotted off, blending into the horizon. The sun reflected off the blue roan's coat, catching the light just right, a beacon urging him forward. But as he rode after his friends, the sense of loss clung to him, a reminder of the bonds they had shared.

Almost clearing the Sioux camp, Challi felt the weight of Odin's gaze upon him. It was a look mixed with disbelief and frustration, a silent plea for him to turn back. "Dammit, I told you to…" Odin started, but his words faded into the wind. Challi knew he was halfway up the mountain, his heart pounding with a mix of defiance and determination. The Dakota Territory was calling him, a land that felt like home even in its harshest conditions.

The rocky terrain of the mountain loomed before him, but Challi pressed on, his resolve strengthening with each step of his horse. Memories of Jolly flooded his mind, laughter shared around campfires and stories that danced in the flickering light. The bond of friendship was like the rope that had tied Shawnee to the mare mule; it could stretch and pull, but it would never break. He could almost hear Jolly's voice urging him to keep going, to embrace the wildness of the journey ahead.

Chapter 15

As he climbed higher, the air grew thinner, and the chill of the mountain seeped into his bones. Yet, the thrill of adventure coursed through his veins. The Sioux camp receded behind him, a reminder of the past, as he ventured into the unknown. Challi felt the weight of the world slipping away, replaced by the freedom of the open sky above and the rugged beauty surrounding him. Every hoof beat resonated with purpose, carrying him closer to a future unwritten.

In the distance, Odin's silhouette grew smaller, but Challi felt no regret. He was forging his own path, one that honored the memory of Jolly while embracing the spirit of the land. The blue roan surged forward, galloping with the wind at its mane, and Challi let out a whoop of exhilaration. He was alive, and this journey—this adventure—was just beginning. With every beat of his heart, he knew he would carry Jolly with him, a guiding light through the wilds of the Dakota Territory.

****

Challi stood at the edge of the Dakota Territory, the sun setting behind the distant hills, casting a golden hue over the land he once called home. After years away, he returned to a place where the whispers of his childhood still lingered among the grass and the wind. But he knew that returning meant facing the harsh reality of living among the white settlers, who regarded him and his kind with suspicion and disdain. He took a deep breath, feeling the weight of his heritage pressing down on his shoulders, yet there was a spark of determination in his heart. He was young and strong, and he was ready to carve out a place for himself in this world.

As Challi made his way into the small settlement, he was met with curious glances from the townsfolk. The children pointed and giggled, their laughter ringing in his ears, while the adults exchanged wary looks. He remembered Old Man Red Feather, a wise elder of the tribe, who had often told him stories of resilience and courage. Challi sought him out, hoping to find comfort and guidance in the familiar warmth of his presence. The old man was seated outside his modest cabin, his face etched with the lines of time, yet his eyes sparkled with wisdom.

"Challi, my boy," Red Feather greeted him, his voice a soothing balm against the harshness of the world. "You have come back to the land of your ancestors. Remember, you carry their strength within you." Challi nodded, feeling a sense of belonging wash over him. They talked for hours, sharing stories of the past and dreams for the future. Red Feather reminded him of the importance of standing tall against prejudice, urging him to find his voice in a world that often silenced those who were different.

Despite the comfort of his conversation with Red
Feather, Challi could not escape the reality of his
surroundings. Sheriff Thompson, a figure of authority in
the town, had long held a grudge against the Native
people. His presence loomed large, casting a shadow
over Challi's attempts to integrate into the community.
One evening, as Challi was helping Odin. The local
sheriff approached them with a scowl.

"What are you doing with that Indian?" Thompson
barked, his tone dripping with disdain. Odin stood his
ground, his eyes narrowing. "Challi is my son, Sheriff.
He has every right to be here, just like you and me."
Challi felt a surge of gratitude for Odin's bravery, but he
also sensed the tension rising between them and the
sheriff. It was a reminder of the chasm that still existed
between their worlds.

Days turned into weeks, and Challi worked hard to
prove himself to the community. He helped build homes,
tended to the fields, and even shared his knowledge of
traditional hunting techniques with those willing to learn.
Slowly, some of the townsfolk began to see him as more
than just an outsider. However, Sheriff Thompson
remained resolute, his disdain unyielding. Challi
understood that change would not come easily, but he
was committed to fostering understanding, one
conversation at a time.

In the quiet moments, Challi often reflected on the
journey before him. He knew that living among the white

settlers would be fraught with challenges, but he also felt a sense of hope igniting within him. With the support of Old Man Red Feather and Odin, he began to envision a future where differences could be celebrated rather than feared. As the sun dipped below the horizon, casting a warm glow over the Dakota Territory, Challi took a deep breath, ready to face whatever lay ahead, determined to bridge the divide and build a life rooted in respect and understanding.

Old Man Red Feather was a man of great wisdom, his weathered face telling stories of his own struggles and triumphs. He often spoke of the importance of understanding one another, of finding common ground despite the barriers that sometimes seemed insurmountable. "Challi," he would say, his voice like a soft breeze, "the world is changing, and so must we. We cannot let fear dictate our choices. Go forth with an open heart, and you may find allies among those you least expect." Challi took these words to heart, feeling a sense of responsibility to honor both his ancestors and the new path he was about to tread.

Odin, a spirited young man with a heart full of dreams, had been Challi's companion since childhood. He shared Challi's vision of a brighter future, one where respect and understanding bridged the gap between their people and the settlers. Together, they had spent countless hours discussing their hopes and fears, always returning to the idea that friendship could transcend any boundary. As they prepared for the journey into the settlers' community, they vowed to support each other, no matter what challenges lay ahead.

As the sun dipped below the horizon, casting a warm golden hue over the landscape, Challi felt a surge of determination. He took a deep breath, filled with the scents of earth and wildflowers, and stepped forward into the unknown. Each step was a reminder that he was not only carrying his own dreams but also the hopes of his tribe. He envisioned conversations that would spark understanding, shared meals that would foster connection, and laughter that would echo across cultural divides.

The first days among the settlers were daunting. Challi faced wary glances and whispered conversations that made his heart race. Yet, he remembered Old Man Red Feather's wisdom and kept his demeanor calm and open. He sought out opportunities to engage with the settlers, offering help in their fields and sharing stories about his people. Slowly, walls began to crumble as curiosity replaced apprehension. Some settlers began to approach him, intrigued by his knowledge of the land and its resources.

Over time, Challi's efforts bore fruit. He found himself welcomed into homes, sharing meals and laughter, forging friendships that transcended cultural boundaries. With Odin by his side, they organized gatherings that celebrated both Dakota traditions and settler customs, allowing both communities to learn from one another. As the seasons changed, so did the hearts of those around him. Challi's journey was not just a personal one; it was a beacon of hope that shone brightly in the Dakota Territory, illuminating the path toward a future where differences could indeed be celebrated rather than feared.

As seasons shifted from the vibrant colors of autumn to the stillness of winter, the gatherings became a regular affair. Families began to bring their children, who played together, weaving friendships that flourished like the new blooms of spring. Each shared meal became a celebration of unity, with Dakota dances blending harmoniously with settlers' folk music. Challi's efforts were not just about coexistence; they were about embracing differences and celebrating the rich tapestry of their shared lives. In this growing friendship, a new chapter began to unfold in the Dakota Territory, where hope glimmered like the first light of dawn on a crisp morning, signaling a future where hearts were open and differences were cherished.

Each gathering was more than just a meeting; it was a celebration of their shared lives. The sounds of Dakota dances mingled with the cheerful notes of settlers' folk music, creating a harmonious blend that filled the air with joy. As they shared meals, each dish told a story of culture and tradition, reminding them that their differences were treasures to be embraced rather than barriers to be feared. With every gathering, hope glimmered like the first light of dawn, hinting at a future rich with understanding and respect, where the hearts of the Dakota people and the settlers beat in unison, creating a vibrant tapestry of life in their beloved territory.

As laughter erupted and shared meals were enjoyed, the barriers between the two cultures began to crumble, revealing a shared humanity that flowed like a river through their gathering. With each dance and every song, Odin and Challi learned that their differences were not walls, but bridges that connected them. The evening sky transformed into a canvas of stars, each twinkling light a promise of hope and understanding for the future. Together, they envisioned a world where their hearts and traditions intertwined, creating a vibrant tapestry of life that celebrated both the Dakota and settler heritages, reminding them that in unity, they found strength and joy.

Milton Keynes UK
Ingram Content Group UK Ltd.
UKHW020406021124
450424UK00014B/1467